At twenty-five, Marji's life ~~~~~~~~~~~~~~~~~~~~~~d. Her newfound faith in God added an extra dimension—a wish to share her Lord with people who did not know Him. Compelled to begin a new ministry in the ghetto, Marji moved from her secure world of wealth into a frightening one of crime and degradation. Amid terrifying threats, angry slumlords, and sullen people, Marji courageously pressed on with her determination to open up a counseling center. Victory over the oppressive influences of the ghetto seemed within her grasp, when a frightening event brought her face-to-face with death and shattered her dream. Find out how Marji challenged the influences of the ghetto in this thrilling story of danger, intrigue . . . and overwhelming faith.

MARJI

JOHN BENTON

SPIRE ⬥ BOOKS

Fleming H. Revell Company
Old Tappan, New Jersey

Scripture quotations are from the King James Version of the Bible.

Library of Congress Cataloging in Publication Data

Benton, John, date
  Marji.

  (A Spire book)
  I. Title.
PZ4.B4788Mar [PS3552.E57]   813'.5'4
ISBN 0-8007-8378-6   79-22058

This is an original Spire book, published by Spire Books, a division of Fleming H. Revell Company, Old Tappan, New Jersey.

To Sally and Carey Girgis

To Sally—for her dedicated leadership and untiring efforts to make this ministry so effective

To Carey—whose Christian example and personal concern lift many a fallen girl

1

I stepped into the elevator and pushed the button for fourteen—all the way to the top. Just as the doors were closing, a boy—about eighteen, I judged—squeezed in. I smiled, but he ignored me. Some people here in New York City just weren't very friendly.

No matter—I leaned back against the rear of the car. I was tired. It would be good to relax at Aunt Joyce's fashionable apartment. The Andrae Crouch concert had been so rewarding, and I knew she would want to hear all about it. Then I'd go to sleep.

I waited for the boy to push the button for his floor, but he just stood there, looking at his feet.

Three, four, five . . . . Maybe he was a delivery boy. Or maybe he was going to see a relative. But he didn't look clean enough or wealthy enough to have relatives in this fancy apartment.

Six, seven . . . . The numbers lighted up. Was he a mugger? Would he try to rape me? I felt my throat tightening. I kept hoping he would reach out and punch ten. Eight, nine, then ten . . . .

I sensed I was in trouble, and I was so scared that I didn't know what to do. If I screamed, would anybody hear me? Or would that make matters worse?

He wasn't even looking my way, so I studied him closely. If anything did happen, there was one thing for sure: I would be able to give the police a description of this mugger.

7

He had on a blue denim jacket and faded blue jeans. His tennis shoes were well worn—there was a hole in the right-hand side of the right shoe. His dark hair hung loosely all around, and he looked as if he was trying to grow a mustache.

Ridiculous! That description could fit thousands of teenagers here in the city.

Then I noticed a scar on his right cheek. It was just barely visible and about two inches long. Good! That would help identify him. He could change clothes; he could shave his half-started mustache. But he couldn't change scars!

It seemed an eternity before we reached fourteen. The elevator doors opened, and he let me step out first. Was he being polite, or . . . ?

Before I could finish the thought, I felt something cold against my throat. A low voice growled, "Okay, lady, one little scream, and I'm jerkin' my hand back. This blade will slice through your neck like Jell-O, and your head is going to fall right at your feet. You understand?"

I was too frightened to answer. I didn't even dare nod my head!

He pushed me down the hall, toward the sign that said EXIT. I knew Aunt Joyce was waiting for me in apartment 1406. The doorman had called her before I started up. If I screamed, she would come running. But that might be the end of me—and of her, too. I decided to keep quiet and try to figure out what he was up to.

He shoved the exit door open. Up a flight of stairs we stumbled, with him shoving me from behind. Then through another door, onto the flat rooftop. I noticed that the full moon gave an eerie glow to the surroundings.

He let his knife down slowly and then wheeled me around. His eyes were full of anger and hate.

"Okay, lady, give me your money. And not one word out of you. You hear?"

I heard! I had about fifty dollars in my purse. Obviously he needed it more than I did. Being a Christian, I had no problem with that. He could have every penny I had. What I wished was that I would get a chance to tell him about Jesus. But would he listen?

I held out my purse. He grabbed it and immediately rifled through my wallet. His dirty hands pulled out the paper money and stuffed it into his pocket.

He checked to see what I was doing. I managed to smile—to try to hide how scared I was. It didn't work.

Next he took the coins out. I remember thinking how I had decided he could have every last penny, and I was angry now that he was taking it! He must be desperate. When he was sure he had all the money, he threw down the wallet and purse.

If I live to be one hundred, I'll never forget what happened next. He planted his feet far apart and raised his knife. Those eyes, partially bloodshot, squinted at me in the moonlight. "Okay, lady, I got your money. Now I want the rest."

"Now listen here, young man," I pleaded. "That's all the money I have. I don't keep any money on my body."

He laughed like a madman. He very deliberately shut his switchblade and stuck it in his pocket. Maybe I'd convinced him . . . .

Then before I knew what was happening, he grabbed

me. I froze. Then with that sinister laugh he whispered, "Lady, I want more than your money."

A surge of fear moved from the pit of my stomach and tightened my throat. It was what I feared the most. Rape!

In a flash I remembered what my father had said: "Now, Marji, you be careful tonight. There are a lot of muggers and rapists in the city, so you be careful."

I shall never forget my answer. "Aw, Dad, I'm twenty-five now. I've been around. Besides, I'm a Christian. God has His angels guarding me. No one can touch me."

"I wouldn't trust my luck to angels, Marji."

I laughed, but he didn't. And where were those angels, now that I needed them?

The boy's hand, trying to rip off my blouse, brought me back to the horror of this moment. Then with all the courage I could muster, I whispered—and I don't really know why—"You look just like my brother, Bucky."

You would have thought I had hit him. He jerked his hand back from my blouse, as if he were touching a hot stove. Then he stepped back and squinted his eyes again.

"What do you mean, I look like your brother? You ain't got no brother like me; I can tell. You even *smell* rich."

What could I tell this boy who had robbed me and who now had rape on his mind? I breathed one of those millionth-of-a-second prayers. I didn't know what had happened to my guardian angels, but I knew I had quick access to God.

"Oh, what I mean is that my brother, Bucky, is real

handsome like you. And another thing about Bucky; he just loves money and girls. I bet you love money and girls, too, don't you?''

Did I detect a small smile?

"Yeah, that's me. Never seem to have enough money and always lookin' for the right girl.''

Now what? I had him talking, but I had to keep the conversation rolling. Somehow if I could get his mind off what he was planning to do to me . . . .

My fear was so great that I almost passed out. I just had to get enough courage to stand up to this young man. If he detected fear, he might strike out in anger. If I said the wrong thing, he might explode.

I took a step toward him, very slowly raised my hand toward his ruffled coat, and began to straighten it and smooth it. He seemed to enjoy that.

It was like what I usually did to Bucky before he left our house. Little brothers loved to be fussed over.

Then I recalled how Bucky always seemed to be reassured when I hugged him. Would it work on this young man?

My parents were very wealthy. Many times they had to be gone, and Bucky and I had to look out for ourselves. Since becoming a Christian, I'd taken a special interest in Bucky. He was eighteen, but the seven years between us didn't seem to matter. We were very close.

But a would-be rapist and a kid brother were two different things! What would he do if I hugged him?

"Mister, do you mind if I ask you something?"

He glared at me. "Now listen here, lady. If you think you're going to ask my name or my address, forget it. You know what else I want, but somehow you're different from any other woman I've been with. Okay, what's your question?''

"You know I mentioned my brother, Bucky? Well, it always seems to help him if I give him a little hug. Now don't get me wrong. I can see you need money, and I'm sure you could probably put it to good use. I know how you feel about girls, and every young man should have good feelings about girls. Someday you'll probably marry and raise a wonderful family. I'm sure you have great potential to be a wonderful husband and father.''

He tried to interrupt, but I kept talking.

"Now a hug always really helped Bucky. Do you mind if I hug you?''

I stared at his mouth—the mouth tells so much. Yes, I did detect a faint smile. And he didn't know what to say.

I moved against him and softly put my arms around him. I squeezed him firmly, then put my hand on the back of his head and pushed his head gently against my shoulder. I felt him relax. He slowly put his arms around me.

There was no passion in the hug, only a big sister's concern for her little brother who had gone astray.

I know the law says that people like this boy should be put in jail. I know that's right. But there is always another side to the story. If you and I had been born in the ghetto and didn't have the advantage of caring parents, where would we be? No money, no love, absolutely nothing! Where would we turn? To survive, we would probably attempt what this young boy turned to: robbing to get money to pay for the necessities of life. And because we'd had no real love, we, too, would probably turn to dirty magazines that cater to the flesh—and rape then seems to be the answer.

I'm not making excuses for deviant behavior, but I know a little bit about what makes people go wrong. My folks had sent me to Radcliffe, and I had studied some psychology. I had even considered a career in social work before Dad insisted that I come into the family business.

We stood there for several minutes on the rooftop. I gently patted his back. Then I felt him release me, and I dropped my hands. We stepped apart.

"Okay, lady. You win this one. I just don't have it in me to go through with it. But I'm keepin' your money. You hear?"

"Listen, let's make a deal. Let's just say I gave you that money. I'm sure you need it more than I do, and I'm glad to help you."

He grinned. "Lady, I don't know what's with you, but you're different. It was easy robbin' you; but that other thing, so help me, I just couldn't do it."

"There is something different about me," I said. "I'm a Christian. God must have been looking out for me."

"You got to be kiddin'! God don't look out for nobody!"

"I know many people feel that way. Millions do, I guess. But just because they feel that way doesn't mean it's true. God will look out for you if you just let Him."

"Okay, lady, answer this one for me."

I smiled. Maybe I would get to witness to him, after

all, to tell him how Jesus had died for his sins and that
there was hope for him. Already I was feeling better.

"I know you rich people," he went on. "You live in
expensive apartments like this one; you drive expensive cars; you buy the latest threads. You don't know
nothin' about bein' poor. You don't know nothin'
about rats and roaches and dirty, filthy tenement
houses. I mean, I bet you never even seen a rat or a
roach in your life, have you?"

That was his question?

"Of course I've seen rats. Anybody who lives in
New York has seen rats. And I've seen roaches. We
have to spray for them all the time. I know what they
look like."

"That's not what I'm gettin' at. I mean, you're sit-
tin' in bed and you feel somethin' bite you. You reach
down and slap at it, and you slap a big rat. That big rat
drops back and begins to hiss at you. You leap out of
bed, screamin'. That's what I'm talkin' about. I been
bitten by dirty rats so many times that I can't count
'em. And, lady, how would *you* like to go to bed in the
middle of winter in a place that's just as cold inside as
outside? I mean, like five degrees above zero, and
you're freezin' to death?

"Now, lady, here's my question: With all the filth
and the rats, with all the robbin' and muggin' and
rapin' and everything else, *where is your God in the
ghetto?*"

Now that was a good question! I couldn't give this
boy a flip answer. Maybe he really was looking for the
truth. Deep within my heart, I searched for an answer.

Where is God in the ghetto?

The boy interrupted my thinking. "One more thing,

lady. I don't know if you're tellin' me the truth about your brother, but I'm going to tell you somethin'. I got a sister named Carmen."

"How old is she?"

"She's twenty-five."

"Oh, really? I'm twenty-five, too."

"How old do you think I am?" he asked.

"Well, my brother, Bucky, is eighteen. Are you eighteen?"

He laughed. "Yeah, I'm eighteen. Coincidence, huh?"

"It sure is."

"Well, let me tell you about Carmen. She ain't like you. She don't wear no fancy clothes. She don't live in no fancy apartment. You see, lady, she's a junkie."

He let that sink in.

"And tonight she's down on Forty-second Street and Eighth Avenue, sellin' her body to support her habit. And, lady, does she ever have a terrible habit! She gets sick, and she's got a real bad disease. It's killin' me to see my own sister out there, actin' that way. I may rob, steal, mug, and do other things, but I ain't no junkie. I know it ain't right to do what I'm doin', but with this money I'm going to buy some heroin for Carmen, so she don't get sick again. Maybe she can get straight. That's why I done it."

I thought I detected a tear glistening on his dirty cheek. I was indeed catching a glimpse of what goes on in the real world. I knew we rich people missed so much. It's one thing to read about these situations; it's quite another to talk to someone who's in the middle of it. There are so many people hurting, not knowing where to turn.

"Now, lady, I'm still waitin' for your answer. Where is your God in the ghetto? Where is your God on Forty-second Street? Where is your God when my sister has to sell her body to support her habit? Where is your God when she has to take a filthy needle and jab it in her arm? Where is your God when I have to walk the street and mug people to get a little cash? Come on, lady. *Where is your God?*"

How could I answer him? Doesn't God care? Why, oh, why, is there all this terrible misery in the world? Where is God in all this, anyway?

O God, somehow give me an answer, I silently prayed.

Then it came, like a flash of inspiration. "Young man, God is everywhere. The Bible tells us that. That includes the ghetto. And that is why He sent His Son, Jesus, to this world. He saw all mankind's problems, and through Jesus He provided a way out. That is why Jesus came. He came to change the world. And He does that by changing people. He wants to change you. He wants to change Carmen. In fact, His love and concern for a world so full of all these sicknesses is so great that Jesus went to the cross to change all this. He died to set people free. That's why He came!

"And right now He is working in all parts of the world to reverse the terrible things that are going on. He has His people on street corners and in churches, telling the world that Jesus really cares.

"But people don't really believe that He cares. They reject His message and stubbornly go on their own way and miss God's purpose for their lives and create all sorts of problems. But Jesus came to change all this."

He stared at me unbelievingly. "Lady, you think you got the answer, don't you? Well, let me ask you one more question. If this Jesus is so great, then how come you're not out on the street, telling my sister about Him?"

I didn't know it then, but that question was destined to change my life!

He really had me. Why *wasn't* I out there? Here I was a Christian, but I was not really doing much about it. My aunt Joyce had won me to the Lord about five years ago, when I was a junior in college. I'd become a member of Campus Crusade for Christ, at my college, but I was better at attending meetings than I was in telling people how Jesus could help them.

Sure, I went to church regularly. I read my Bible every day and prayed. But I was kind of afraid to witness to anyone.

Then, too, I didn't get much encouragement at home. My parents weren't Christians. Dad owned Parker Manufacturing Company. He had offices around the world, with headquarters here in New York City. He didn't object to my being a Christian. It was more as if he humored me—treated it as if it were a phase, something I would grow out of when I became more mature.

It was always his dream for me to become involved in the company. I guess that's why he insisted I start to work there after I finished college.

But business life never really did appeal to me. I still didn't know what I wanted to do with my life, but I enjoyed working in the fashion-design department of Dad's company.

The boy asked me again: "Lady, how come you're

not out on the streets tellin' people about this Jesus?"

"I'll have to be honest with you," I said slowly. "I really don't have an answer."

He started toward the door that led inside. Just then he turned, and my heart skipped another beat. "Lady, you're lucky. You don't know how lucky you are. The last time I got a girl and got what I wanted, I took my knife and cut her face!"

He disappeared, and I stood there in that eerie moonlight. I pinched myself. Surely this must be a bad dream. I would wake up and . . . .

Then all the pent-up fear rushed to the surface, and I began to shake uncontrollably. Then came the sobs—great, deep ones. Big tears gushed down my cheeks.

I had been spared the indecency of rape. I had been spared getting cut up. Was it luck? Or had God's guardian angels really been watching over me?

My emotions were all mixed up. First, I felt relief, then anger. How dare he do this to an upright citizen? What's the matter with people like that anyway?

But then I could hear his voice telling me about the rats and the roaches and about his junkie sister. How could I blame somebody who had so many strikes against him?

The more I thought about it, the more I cried. But not out of fear. This was a cry for people hurting. What could I do to help them?

I waited for a few more minutes and then slowly walked over and opened the door. I couldn't see him anywhere. So I hurried down the steps to apartment 1406. Aunt Joyce would be worried sick. I didn't know how long that boy had kept me out on the roof, but it was long enough for her to be worried.

I had gone to the Andrae Crouch concert at the Felt Forum at Madison Square Garden. Then, as my dad had said, I had taken a taxi to my aunt's apartment house on the East Side.

I knocked on 1406—no answer. I knocked again—nothing. Where was Aunt Joyce? Had the mugger forced his way into her apartment and . . . ? What if he came back now?

I knocked again, harder. Then I kicked—still no answer.

Panic hit me. I glanced at the elevator and saw it was coming up. Oh, no! What could I do now? There was no place to hide!

I pounded and pounded. Why didn't she answer?

Then the elevator stopped, and the doors flew open. I started to run down the hall.

"Marji! Marji! Stop! Stop!"

I recognized that voice.

"Aunt Joyce," I screamed. "Where have you been?"

"What do you mean? Where have *you* been? I've been out of my mind worrying about you."

Now she was close enough to see me clearly. "Marji!" she shrieked. "What has happened to you? Look at your blouse. It's ripped! You look awful!"

I tried to tell her I had been robbed and almost raped. But all I could do was to fall into her arms and sob.

She hugged me close. "There, there," she said. "Tell Aunt Joyce what happened."

"I was robbed and almost raped!"

"Oh, no! Are you hurt?"

"No, I'm okay. Thank God, my life was spared."

She tightened her arms around me. "Marji, I read so much in the papers about robbing and raping, but I never did think it would happen to my dear niece."

I then told her how the boy had forced me out onto the rooftop. She turned white as a sheet. "And to think it happened in this very building," she said. "No place is safe anymore!"

We walked over to her door, and she turned the handle. "Oh, no! I've locked myself out. I kept waiting and waiting for you. I thought maybe you had stopped to see some friends on another floor, although that wasn't really like you. Then I heard some noises out in the hallway. I opened the door, but no one was there. I decided to go down to the entrance to see if you had gone back outside or something. The guard said he had seen you come in, but that you hadn't gone out. That's when I really got scared."

"While all that was going on, I was up on the roof."

"Well, Marji, you're safe now. I'll go down to the doorman and borrow his master key. You stay right here."

"Safe? Staying here? I'm not going to stay anywhere by myself. That boy may come back!"

"You're right. You'd better come with me."

"But we'll have a problem with that doorman. He knows you were looking for me, and he's going to ask what happened when he sees the way I look. Then he'll call the cops. I can just see the headline in tomorrow's *Daily News*: HENRY PARKER'S DAUGHTER ESCAPES RAPE ATTEMPT! Dad would flip out. He'd never let me go anywhere again. And it would be bad for him and his business. People would be crawling all over the place for the story.''

"You're right again. But what can we do? I can't leave you here.''

"I'll take my chances with the doorman.''

We took the elevator down. I kept close to it while Aunt Joyce walked over to the doorman and asked to borrow the master key.

"Find your niece?" he asked.

"Yes, she's okay. You know these young people. But I locked myself out of my apartment in all the rush.''

He said he would come up and open the door for her, but Aunt Joyce declined his offer. He saw me standing by the elevator. Fortunately the lights weren't too bright there. I tried to act nonchalant. I don't know what he was thinking, but I guess he assumed it would be best if he didn't ask any more questions.

We got the key and unlocked the apartment. I stepped inside, and Aunt Joyce said, "Now lock the door. I'll return this key and be right back.''

I locked it and bolted it and chained it and put a chair up against it. There was no way that boy was going to get me now!

In a few minutes Aunt Joyce was back. I guess she wasn't too surprised at how long it took me to open the door for her, not after what I had been through.

We sat down on the sofa together, and I told her the whole story again. When I had finished, she started for the phone.

"I'd better call your folks and tell them you're safe and alive.''

I jumped up. "Please, Aunt Joyce, don't call Mom

and Dad. They don't know what's happened here.
They think I'm safe in your apartment. You know that
Dad would never let me come here again if he found
out what happened."

"Well, your dad may be right. This city is no place
for a girl like you."

Then it was just as if I were seeing that boy again, on
instant replay, and hearing him ask, "If this Jesus is so
great, then how come you're not out on the street,
telling people about Him?"

I told Aunt Joyce about it. And I added, "Please
don't ever say again that the city is no place for me.
For the first time in my life, I've gotten a little glimpse
of the way people hurt in this city. They desperately
need help. Maybe I ought to be out there on the
streets, telling them about Jesus. So please don't tell
my dad what happened here tonight."

"Marji," she responded, "you're not thinking
about . . . . Oh, no! You wouldn't . . . . Or would
you?"

"I really don't know what or how, Aunt Joyce. I
know God didn't cause this terrible thing to happen,
but I think that through it all maybe He is getting a
message across to me."

She studied me quizzically. Maybe she thought it
was an emotional reaction to the fear. But I still
couldn't get away from that boy's searching question.
And I still didn't have any answer for him. But I felt an
excitement, as if I was on the verge of a great discovery!

2

Maybe God was saying something to me through that awful experience. But I must admit it still left me visibly shaken, and Aunt Joyce finally insisted that I get some rest.

I always read my Bible before going to sleep, and for my devotions I had turned to Psalm 116. I had just started the eighth verse, "For thou hast delivered my soul from death . . . ," when Aunt Joyce knocked on my door.

"Come on in."

"Marji, I saw your light was still on. I couldn't sleep, and I figured maybe you couldn't either. I just remembered a book I bought a few weeks ago that has something to do with what we were talking about. It's called *Cindy,* and it's the story of a girl drug addict."

"Now don't tell me you are studying how to become a junkie?"

Aunt Joyce laughed. "No, not quite. But this is one of the most interesting stories I've ever read. It tells about a girl who became a drug addict, had a child out of wedlock, and then had to give up that child—the only thing she'd ever loved—because of her habit. It's such a tragic story, but it has a fantastic ending. The girl gave her heart to Christ and went to a place called the Walter Hoving Home, upstate."

"Walter Hoving Home?" I asked. "Isn't that the Teen Challenge girls' home in Garrison, New York? I remember my pastor saying something about it. And I read a feature on it in the newspaper."

"Yes, that's it. They have a tremendous program for helping girls, and it's fantastically successful, I understand. They use the Scriptures to teach girls how to live."

As she handed me the book, I glanced at the cover. It showed a girl— I judged she was about my age— holding her young daughter. My heart went out to her. It was such a pathetic sight! Thank God there was hope for someone like this!

"One more thing, Marji. I'm probably making a mistake giving you that book tonight. If you're like me, if you start it, you won't be able to put it down. It will keep you up all night!"

"Oh, that's okay, Aunt Joyce. I still feel kind of jittery. I think I need something to calm me down."

"That book won't calm you down! At least, it didn't calm me. The night I read it, I got so excited that I couldn't sleep the rest of the night!"

Aunt Joyce hugged me and said, "Marji, I just wanted to tell you again how much I love and appreciate you. You know you're my favorite niece. I guess I shouldn't have favorites, but you've always been extra special to me, ever since you took Jesus as your Saviour."

Aunt Joyce was so sweet and so understanding and helpful.

"There's something else I think I should say," she continued. "There must be a reason why God spared your life tonight. Don't ever forget to thank Him for that. And keep open to Him."

That brought my tears again.

"There, there," she said as she hugged me close. "I didn't mean to start those tears all over."

"It's not that. I'm just so confused. Dad wants me to learn the business, but I really feel I ought to be doing more for the Lord."

"God will show you the way, Marji. Trust Him. Now you get some rest."

She closed the door. I was about to turn off the light when my eye caught the cover of *Cindy* again. I told myself I would read for a few minutes, until I got sleepy.

But Aunt Joyce was right! Once I started it, I couldn't put it down.

Cindy was a poor girl who went to the very bottom with her habit of drug addiction. She had been beaten up by pimps, thrown in jail time after time, and lost all her dignity and respect.

One of the saddest parts was the episode in which Cindy had to go to the welfare department to give up her little daughter, Melodie. Cindy could no longer care for her because of her problem of drug addiction. Yes, that mother had to give up the only love of her life, her little daughter. As I read, I could almost hear Melodie screaming for her mother to come back.

Then one day Cindy wandered into a church and heard a girl who had graduated from the Walter Hoving Home tell how Christ had set her free. The message didn't get through, because Cindy, in total despondency, headed back to her filthy apartment to take a gun and kill herself.

But two people from the church followed her and stopped her suicide attempt. They got her out of the city and up to the Walter Hoving Home, where she accepted Christ as her Saviour.

I was glad I kept reading. The story ended so beautifully. Cindy is now reunited with Melodie and living for the Lord. What a fantastic miracle!

When I finished the book, I glanced at the clock. Four o'clock in the morning. How time flew!

I flipped off the light, but I still couldn't sleep. The memory of Cindy haunted me. True, one Cindy had been helped. But how many more Cindys were still wandering the streets, living in filth, prostituting their bodies, and being abused by perverts and pimps? Didn't anyone care? Did I care?

While I was in a nice, warm bed in a luxurious apartment overlooking the Hudson River, girls were out there committing unbearable acts to support their habits.

I had everything a girl could want: an education at Radcliffe, a well-paying job in my dad's business, a career with a future so bright I would end up as a millionaire. I lived in a gorgeous mansion on Long Island and had a chauffeured Cadillac at my disposal. I had everything. Then why did I have this vague, un-easy feeling that there was something wrong with my life? After all, a Christian is supposed to be content.

I rolled over and buried my face in the pillow. It didn't seem fair that I had so much while others had so little. I was warm; they were cold. I was secure; they were living in fear. I had hope; they had despair. Girls wandering the streets of the city, with no future what-ever.

I felt so guilty that I sobbed.

But what could I do? Even though I had a good education, I really didn't know how to reach these people. We lived in two different worlds. Would they listen to me? Would they trust me? Would they ever accept me? Wouldn't it be better to let converted girls like Cindy try to reach them? They would know she understood. What could *I* possibly understand about their heartaches and suffering and despair?

I don't know how long I cried, but eventually I must have dozed off, because I was awakened by a persistent knock on the door.

I slowly rolled over and tried to open my eyes. Oh, I felt awful! I finally mumbled, "Yes?"

The door opened, and there stood Aunt Joyce, smiling and holding a breakfast tray. "Well, my little darling, I thought it was time for you to get up."

"What time is it?"

"It's ten-thirty."

That late? I was awake now! "My goodness, I didn't know it was that late!"

"Well, that was a terrible episode last night. I figured you needed to rest. Oh, by the way, your father called at nine and wanted to talk to you."

"You didn't tell him what happened last night, did you?"

"No, but I think you should."

"I can't! If he knew, he'd never let me come into the city again. He has no use for people in the ghetto, anyway."

"Well, I've been praying for your father. Jesus can change him, too."

"That's something I like about you, Aunt Joyce. You believe that nothing is too hard, that the Lord will always answer."

"Come on, Marji, eat. And, yes, I believe that God

performs miracles. It looks as if He's going to have to perform a miracle on you this morning. Your eyes are all puffy. Didn't you sleep?''

"It was that book you gave me. It kept me up until four.''

"I warned you!'' she teased. Then she added, "John Benton, the head of the Walter Hoving Home, has written some other books, too. You should read *Carmen*. That will keep you up, too.''

"Not tonight, please. Somewhere along the line I'm going to have to get some sleep!''

We both laughed. "You'd better hurry with that breakfast,'' she said. "Your father is sending Harry to pick you up in an hour. We don't have much time to solve all your problems!''

Harry was our chauffeur. He'd worked for Dad for twenty years, and Bucky and I always felt as if he were one of the family. We teased him and called him Hairy Harry. He really was a wonderful guy and treated us as if we were the only kids in the world.

"Your father wants you out at the Belmont Racetrack this afternoon. He's just bought a new horse, and he wants to show it off.''

Dad had a crazy interest in racehorses. I guess he had so much money that he didn't know what to do with it, so he bought expensive horses. I loved the horses, but I wasn't all that interested in the racetrack.

"After Harry picks you up, you're to go back home for your mother and Bucky and then out to Belmont.''

After breakfast I fixed my face as best I could. It

wasn't long until the doorman called to say that Harry was waiting.

I kissed Aunt Joyce good-bye and made her promise again that what happened last night would be our secret.

Harry opened the door, and I got into the backseat. He wasn't comfortable if we rode in front. He didn't think that was befitting the dignity of a chauffeur!

As we started home, I said, "Harry, would you do me a favor? Could we go down to the Lower East Side and drive through the ghetto?"

"The Lower East Side?" he asked. "Are you sure?"

"We'll be safe, won't we?"

"Of course, we'll be safe. But why in the world do you want to drive through the Lower East Side? Do you know what that part of the city looks like?"

"That's just it, Harry. I've never been there. I'm twenty-five, and I think it's time that I see what it's really like."

Without another word, Harry headed down FDR Drive. We got off at Houston Street, and he drove over to Avenue B. He turned right and went up to Sixth Street. Then he turned left, and we were in the middle of hell.

Everyone was staring at us. A chauffeured Cadillac apparently wasn't something that happened every day on the Lower East Side.

I saw the burned-out tenements and broken-down buildings. But I saw something else: people wandering aimlessly with that hollow look of despair on their faces—broken-down lives! How my heart ached for them. How could people live in such squalor, almost next door to wealth? It hit me that New York City was a city of tremendous contrasts. It has its rich; it has its poor. It has some of the best brains in the world and some people who can't read or write.

I was glad the light was red. It gave me a minute to study a girl to my right. She was standing there, scratching her face. She was skinny and, at first glance, kind of attractive. I'd read that junkies scratch to get a better feeling when they get high.

"Harry, over there on the right, see that girl scratching? Is she a junkie?"

"Yep."

We were only fifteen feet from her. I could see now she really wasn't attractive. Maybe she had been, once. Her eyes were half-open and kind of sunk back in her head. She looked so frail.

She glanced my way, and I smiled. Almost involuntarily, I guess, she smiled back.

My heart exploded. *Oh, God,* I prayed silently, *please, please do something to help that poor girl! She looks so sick, so tired, so lost. If only somehow she could be touched by Your love!*

I wanted to leap out of our limousine and throw my arms around her and tell her that Jesus loved her and that I loved her, too—that there was hope. I wanted to tell her that her sins could be forgiven and she could experience peace. I wanted to tell her that I cared and that, most of all, Jesus cares.

Those thoughts so overwhelmed me that I put my head against the window and began to sob. I thought about Cindy. I thought about that boy who had tried to rape me. I thought about his sister out there, selling her body to support her habit, and about the thousands upon thousands of people who were walking the streets of this great city without any hope. There had to be an answer for these girls.

Harry turned around. "Marji, what's the matter? Is it too much for you down here?"

"Oh, Harry, doesn't it do something to you to see a girl like that?"

"You don't know how much it does, Marji. I've never told any of your family this, but I had a sister who died of an overdose, years ago. Many times I've wept over her death. I told myself I wasn't the brother I ought to have been."

I had no idea that drug addiction had hit Harry's life, too. You never know the deep hurts people have.

"Harry, I'm so sorry. I just wish I could do something."

"I know how you feel. But it's too late now. You know what? She died sitting on the steps of a church! Now, I'm not blaming the church, but it's a puzzle to me that the churches don't seem to be doing their job. Doesn't God care about these people?"

I noticed a tear trickle down Harry's cheek before he abruptly turned away from me.

"Oh, Harry, I know God cares. But He works through people. He needs someone to go out among these people and tell them about Jesus. I've even thought maybe I should. But I'm really in no position to understand and help them. But I do care."

I glanced back to where the girl had been standing. The light had changed, and she was gone. I thought about jumping out to try to find her, but Harry had started moving with the traffic.

I fell back into the seat and began to pray: *God, please do something about that girl. Help her.*

It's hard to describe what happened next. I can't say I actually heard the voice of God, but a still small voice came back to my mind with a question: "Why don't *you* do something about it?"

I began to argue with God. I told Him I wasn't capable. I explained I had come from a too-sophisticated background to come to a place like this. I told God how my father wanted me to learn his business and would never give me permission to come down here. Besides, these people would never trust me.

But no matter what I said, I couldn't get away from that searching question: "Why don't *you* do something about it?"

By this time we were back on FDR Drive headed north. Harry was busy with his own thoughts, and I think he sensed I wanted to be alone with mine. It gave me time to think and to pray and to make up my mind that somehow, some way, I *was* going to do something about it. My interest and studies in social work wouldn't go to waste. I could tie it together with telling people in the ghetto about Jesus!

My biggest hurdle, I decided, would be my father. He wouldn't understand. He would consider my life a waste. He would be disappointed if I didn't go into the business. He'd flip if he even knew I'd asked Harry to drive me through the Lower East Side. And he'd go into a rage if he learned I had been robbed and nearly raped!

I decided there must be some hidden reason why I had never been allowed to go to the Lower East Side. Once, at dinner, we had had a conversation about it.

An acquaintance had a business down there, and I told Dad I wanted to go down and see what kind of order he'd give us. Dad jumped to his feet and screamed, "Don't ever go down to the Lower East Side! It's one of the worst places in America!"

After dinner I mentioned to Mother that Dad's reaction had seemed so unreasonable. She didn't think so!

As we drove along, I decided to see if Harry knew anything about our family and the Lower East Side. Chauffeurs don't talk much, but they hear a lot.

"Harry, has my family ever mentioned the Lower East Side to you?"

"No. Why?"

"Well, several years ago we were discussing it at dinner, and my dad had a violent reaction to the subject. Mom went into a tizzy, too. I remember thinking they almost seemed as if they were trying to hide something."

Harry didn't say a word.

I decided to try again.

"Harry, you didn't answer me directly. Is there something about my family and the Lower East Side?"

No answer.

By this time we had crossed the Triborough Bridge and were headed for Locust Valley, on the north side of Long Island. That's where our estate was.

I leaned forward and touched Harry's shoulder. "If there's something about our family and the Lower East Side, you can tell me. I promise I won't breathe a word to anybody about it."

Still no answer.

"Harry, your silence tells me that something is up

about the Lower East Side. If you don't tell me, I'm going to go to my dad and demand an answer!"

Harry eased the Cadillac to the side of the road, stopped, and turned to face me. "Marji, if I tell you something, you must promise never to tell anyone I told you. This could cost me my job. Do you promise?"

I nodded.

"It has to do with your uncle Alex."

"Uncle Alex? He's in Germany heading up a huge manufacturing company. We haven't seen him in years."

Harry hung his head. "That's not the truth, Marji. That's what your folks want you to believe."

"Uncle Alex *isn't* in Germany?"

"No, Marji. Your uncle Alex is in the Lower East Side, living in drunkenness and poverty."

"Come on, Harry; you don't mean to tell me that my own parents have been lying to me all these years?"

"I'm afraid so, Marji. And it's always bothered me. I think you're old enough to know the truth. I think you have a right to know how it happened. But remember, you promised not to tell that I told you!"

3

Harry was about to reveal some deep, dark family secret!

"Marji," he began, "do you remember when your grandfather Parker died?"

"Grandfather Parker? Oh, I loved him. He was always so generous. He bought my first pony and my first bicycle. I was little when he died, but, yes, I remember it."

"Well, after your grandfather Parker died, there was a big blowup in your family concerning his will. Probably you were too young to remember, but your uncle Alex and your grandfather never did get along too well. Your father was always your grandfather's favorite son. I suppose you might say that your father, Henry, was the good one and Alex was the bad one."

"Well, I did know that Uncle Alex had been married three times. The last time I saw him at our place, he was with a very young woman. And I overheard my folks talking about how he drank too much and was always chasing women."

"Alex didn't have any business sense," Harry continued. "He simply enjoyed spending money. Your grandfather tried to take him into the business, but he finally had to fire him. Every once in a while Alex would threaten to commit suicide."

"Did he ever try it?"

"Yes, but everybody covered it up. One night he staggered into your father's house, with his wrists slashed. Rather than rush him to a hospital and have the thing blown up in the newspapers, your dad called the doctor to the house. Alex later admitted he did it to get even with your grandfather.

"Well, after your grandfather died and the will was read, I guess Alex flipped out. Your grandfather left Alex ten percent of the estate and gave ninety percent to your father. Alex was so angry that he threatened to jump off the Empire State Building."

"But why would Grandfather do something like that? It seems terribly unfair."

"In his will your grandfather gave his reasons. He said that if he gave it to Alex and Henry fifty-fifty, Alex would spend his half and ruin the business, and nothing would be left. He was sure right about that."

"Then what happened to Uncle Alex?"

"He kept making noises and threats. Reporters started getting onto it, and it became a real embarrassment to your father. Of course, Alex took his ten percent, and it wasn't long before he had squandered it. He came back and begged more from your father, and your father tried to help him along. Alex drank more and more. He finally ended up in the Bowery as an alcoholic.

"I know it really hurt your father to see his own brother end up that way. I know he sends him five hundred dollars a month down there, where he lives on the Lower East Side. But there's been absolutely no contact between them, other than that monthly check."

"But why did my folks make up this big lie about his being a successful businessman in Germany?"

"Well, your father and your uncle Alex have an understanding. Because Alex is an embarrassment to

the family and to the business, your father will pay him
five hundred dollars a month if he stays down on the
Lower East Side. If he tries to make contact with your
family or with the press, he'll be cut off immediately.''

"But I still don't understand why Mom and Dad
don't want Bucky and me to know about it.''

"They're embarrassed, Marji. And they know you.
Now just suppose for a moment that you knew your
uncle Alex was down on the Bowery. Knowing you
and Buck, I know what you'd do right away; you'd go
looking for him. Then you'd do just what you used to
do with all the stray puppies and kittens—you'd want
to bring him home and take care of him. Here your
father is trying to forget about Alex, and you'd be
reminding him of Alex and his horrible life. Your parents want to forget the whole mess.''

Harry sure knew me well. Already I was wondering
if there was a way I could find Uncle Alex. After all,
he was my uncle, and he needed help. Most of all, he
needed Jesus.

"Harry, you've got to help me find him!''

"So help me, Marji, I knew I shouldn't tell you.
Listen to me! If your dad knew I was telling you this
story, I wouldn't last until five tonight! Then *I* might
have to go down to the Lower East Side and live on
welfare. You wouldn't want that to happen to me,
would you? So you'd better remember what you promised me, and cool it!''

He had me. Certainly, after all Harry had done for
me, I couldn't go to my father and tell him I knew
about Uncle Alex. There had to be some other way.

"Okay, Harry, I promised I wouldn't tell. I won't.
You can count on my word.''

Satisfied, he turned and started the engine and glided into the traffic toward home. Neither of us said any more.

I leaned back and thought about what Harry had told me. Here I wanted to help people in the ghetto, and now I had learned that my own uncle lived there and needed help. Only I wasn't supposed to know that. What could I do? Probably nothing, unless . . . .

When we got home, Mom and Bucky were waiting. "What took you so long?" she asked as she gave me a little hug. I wondered if Aunt Joyce had told her about last night. But she didn't show any unusual concern, only a little annoyance that we had kept them waiting.

"Oh, Mom, you know the traffic in New York City . . . ."

"Yes, I know," she interrupted. "I also know that your father will be getting mighty impatient for us to see that new horse. Let's hurry to Belmont, Harry."

At the stables Dad was waiting impatiently, just as Mother had predicted. "What took you so long?" he asked. But before we could answer, he began to tell us about the tremendous new racehorse he had just bought. "Come on!" he said. "You've got to see my prize possession!" He was like a kid with a new toy.

But Dad was right: This was a beautiful horse. Maybe even a Kentucky Derby winner, someday.

I walked over and petted the horse. He had that firmness about him that was so necessary for a winner. His muscles were well toned, and Dad said he had had excellent training.

After convincing Dad that we were thoroughly impressed with his new horse, we all went our separate

ways. I wandered around and chatted with some of my
old friends at the stables. I did love horses and enjoyed
being around the grooms and the jockeys. I used to kid
Dad that I was around the stables so much that I'd
probably marry a jockey. He'd laugh, but I think it
made him a little nervous. He was so particular about
the kind of fellows I dated.

I was getting a little hungry, so I decided to head
back to where Dad was. Maybe he'd take me to the
club for a sandwich.

Dad was busy brushing his new horse. Even though
he hired grooms, he still liked to pitch in and do some
of the work himself. He was always that way about
everything.

When he spotted me alone, before I could say anything, he asked, "Got a minute?"

I held my breath. Whenever he asked, "Got a minute?" I knew something important was coming.
Maybe Aunt Joyce felt she had to tell him about last
night!

He put the brush down and paced back and forth in
the stall. "There's something on my mind, Marji—
something I've been giving a lot of thought to these
past few months. And I've now come to a decision. I
know you'll be excited about it."

He was using his psychology on me!

Then, putting his arm around my shoulder, he said,
"Why don't we go over to the club and have a cup of
coffee? I'll tell you what I have in mind when we get
there. Okay?"

"Dad, we don't need to go anywhere. You can tell
me here."

"Oh, no, Marji. This is going to take a little time to

explain. I mean, this is really something."

"Like, man, real heavy?"

He smiled. He was an easy one to jive. "Yeah, man," he said. "Dig it!"

We both laughed. "Okay, I'll go with you if you order me something besides coffee. I'm starved."

In a few moments we were at the clubhouse and ordered our coffee and sandwiches.

Then Dad broke the news. "Marji, I've been giving some serious thought to retiring."

"Dad, you're not even fifty yet!" I broke in. "You're not planning to head for a rocking chair already, are you?"

He laughed his strong firm laugh. "Of course not, honey. But because of the company, I've got to start making plans now. I can't wait until the last minute. Parker Manufacturing is a solid organization. I think it's been properly managed, well capitalized, and has a tremendous growth pattern. I want to keep it that way."

"So?"

"You don't understand, do you? I need to make plans for what will happen to the company when I'm not around."

"You'll be around, Dad. And then just pick a good man to follow you and train him. That's all."

He looked me straight in the eye. "Marji, I'm not looking for a good man. I want *you* to take over the company!"

I almost fell out of my chair. There had been hints of this before; but here it was, finally, out in the open. And it was absolutely stupid!

"Dad, do you know what you're saying? How could

a twenty-five-year-old woman like me take over Parker Manufacturing? You must be out of your mind!''

He reached over and patted my hand. ''Calm down, Marji, and let me explain.''

This was going to be interesting!

''Since you've been working in design, I have had some of my people keep a close eye on you. We had a preplanned program to see how much responsibility you could take. Everything has been going according to plan.''

''Plan? What plan? I was just doing my job. I've enjoyed it, but you've paid me good money to do it.''

''You've been doing more than I'm paying you to do. Remember when we sent you to Paris to look at the latest fashions with Amelia Baruch? I told Amelia to be sure you made some of the major decisions. You did, and you came through with flying colors. The fashions you picked were the ones that really sold. We made a lot of money because of your decisions, and you'll be getting a nice bonus, next week, because of that.''

''Thanks, but I was just doing my job.''

''Something else. Remember when Otto Kramer was having a lot of personnel problems? We sent him to you. That report you wrote was absolutely amazing. You not only solved Otto's problems, but you helped him become one of our most productive supervisors!''

''Dad, I don't think it was fair of you to be testing me all the time. If I had known those people were watching over my shoulder, I would have quit.''

''Exactly, Marji, so don't be upset with me. I knew I couldn't tell you. But I had to find out if you were really executive material. And I mean *chief* executive.

Based on what you have done, I have decided that you can be trained to be the next president of Parker Manufacturing."

"Dad, that is absolutely nuts. There is no way I can run that company. It's a worldwide operation. So I made a few right decisions. I still don't know anything about management. I majored in social work."

"Oh, I know you can't take over tomorrow, or even next year. What I have in mind is a planned program toward your eventually assuming the presidency. You'll work in the various departments to learn all the operations. You know, I think a boss should know how to do the work! Then by the time you are thirty, you should be able to assume some management responsibility. And within ten years of that, by the time I'm sixty-five, you'll be making all the decisions. Oh, Marji, I just know you'll do a tremendous job with the company. I'll be so proud of you!"

I hadn't wanted to say anything yet about what God was talking to me about. I really needed more time to think and to pray about it. Yet Dad had brought me to this crossroad. It wouldn't be fair not to level with him now.

"Dad, I'm honored that you have so much confidence in me. And you know I've always tried to make you proud of me. But there is something else you need to know. Lately some events have changed my view of this world and my place in it."

Dad stared. "Don't tell me you're planning to become a hippie?" He laughed.

"Oh, Dad, hippies aren't 'in' anymore. That was years ago."

"Oh, then it's got something to do with your religion. You're going to smuggle Bibles into Russia.''

"Dad, please be serious. You think I'd be good at that?''

"You sure would! With your looks and brains, you could do anything you set your mind to!''

We both laughed, and it broke the tension. But I knew it wasn't a time for joking. I had to tell him.

"Let me get right to the point, Dad. I have decided to go down to the Lower East Side and establish a counseling center to help girls who are addicts and prostitutes.''

Counseling center? I really hadn't even considered that, myself, until the words were out of my mouth. Maybe the Lord really was directing me.

But when Dad heard what I said, his jaw dropped and he jumped up from the table. "Addicts and prostitutes?'' he thundered.

Naturally everyone else in the clubhouse turned and stared at us. When Dad realized that, he slowly sank back into his chair, leaned toward me, and half-whispered, "Now let me understand this. You want to go down to the Lower East Side and help the addicts and prostitutes?''

"That's right, Dad.''

"Marji, you've had a lot of Pollyanna ideas in your lifetime, but this is the most harebrained yet. Do you have any idea what you would be getting into? And what makes you think those junkies would listen to a little rich girl? You may have taken a degree in sociology, but those people down there would laugh you right out of town!''

"Dad, I really didn't want to talk to you about this yet. I needed more time to think it over. But you forced me to bring it up. Now all I know is that there are people down there who are hurting, and no one seems to care. I want to tell them that Jesus cares.''

"How are you going to help them? give them money? The government's been doing that for years. It doesn't work!"

"I want to give them something worth more than money, Dad. If they take what I give them, they will become responsible citizens." Then I added quietly, "I want to give them Jesus."

"Oh, come on, Marji. A religious *do-gooder* isn't going to change the ghetto. It's been tried."

Dad was getting so upset that I knew it was useless to try to reason with him. So I decided to hit something else head-on.

"What's bothering you the most, Dad? Is it that I'm not taking the presidency? Is it that you don't like addicts and prostitutes? Or is there something about the Lower East Side that you're afraid of?"

I waited. I especially watched for his reaction to my last question. Would he tell me about Uncle Alex?

"Marji, naturally I'm terribly disappointed that you won't take the presidency. For years your mother and I have worked hard. I've committed myself to the success of the company. There were times I would rather have spent with you, but I rationalized that it was all for you, anyway. I don't want to see the company crumble and die. And so far Buck shows no interest in it whatsoever."

"Dad, I know you've worked hard. You and Mother have been so good to me, and I don't mean to sound unappreciative. But, Dad, I've got to do something else with my life. God has first claim on me. And I think He wants me to go down to the Lower East Side and help those people. Dad, what about those poor girls who are addicts and prostitutes? Do you ever think about the horrible life they lead?''

''Well, it's not the kind of thing I spend a lot of time thinking about, Marji. But sometimes I do. I worried about the drug problems when you and Buck were in high school. And every so often a colleague will confide in me about a drug problem within his family. I've seen some of those men break down and cry. I'm so happy you never got into that scene, and it seems as if Buck is okay.''

''All right, Dad, but what's the matter with the Lower East Side? Are you afraid of it?''

Dad twirled his empty coffee cup, studying it closely. Then slowly he looked at me. Maybe he was going to tell me about Uncle Alex!

''Yes, Marji, I'm afraid of the Lower East Side. It's being overtaken by crime, delinquency, murder, rape, and all kinds of evils. I really think we businessmen should begin to pour our money and talents into restoring the Lower East Side to its capabilities.''

He had evaded my question or at least the intent of my question. I decided to push harder. ''Is that all you think about the Lower East Side? Just about businesses and old buildings? What about the people who live there in filth, in misery, in disappointment? Some have been cut off from society and live like the rats and roaches that infest the Lower East Side. They're in horrible poverty. Some are sick. All are hopeless.''

''Well, don't blame me for that. That's their tough luck. I didn't put them there, and I don't feel guilty about the way they live. If they had any ambition . . . .''

"Dad, please don't talk that way," I interrupted. "Have you ever been down to the Lower East Side? Have you ever looked into the hopeless eyes of those people?"

"Come on, Marji. You don't really know what it's like down there. Maybe all your studies have made you feel guilty about those people, but don't try to put the weight of their problem on me. It's not *my* fault!"

Dad fumbled with his coffee cup again. There was a long pause, until I finally said, "Dad, look at me."

He slowly raised his head. "Dad, it isn't a matter of putting the blame on somebody. Those people need help *now*. And can you honestly tell me that, out of the hundreds of thousands of people on the Lower East Side, you don't care about even one of them? not a single, solitary one?"

He sat there, just staring at his coffee cup. I felt so sorry for him. I knew he was thinking about Uncle Alex and the misery he was going through. Some people think that successful businessmen like my dad don't have any emotions. But they do. They hurt. They cry. They love. Dad was hurting now, but I couldn't tell him I knew why.

I wanted to reach over and hug him and tell him there was hope for his future and the company, if he would trust God. God would send the right person to run the company. And God could heal the breach between him and Uncle Alex. Oh, if only my dad would take Jesus as his Saviour! If Uncle Alex would, too! That would be such a miracle.

And I knew it would take a miracle for Dad to let me go through with my plans for the Lower East Side. I

just had to have his approval. I knew the Lord wanted
me to obey my parents, and I didn't want to go down
there without their blessing.

Big tears were forming in Dad's eyes and slowly
trickling down his cheeks. It was the first time I remembered seeing my father cry.

I moved over and put my arms around him. People
were watching, but I didn't care. He was my dad, and I
loved him very much. And I knew why he was crying.

When he finally regained his composure, he stood up
and said, "Marji, I'm not taking your decision as final.
I will discuss this with your mother and give you an
answer tomorrow."

I wanted to ask, "Answer on what? Whether I become president of the company? Whether I can go to
the Lower East Side? or even something about Uncle
Alex?" But his voice had a note of finality to it, and I
knew I shouldn't say anything further.

Just as Dad and I stepped outside the clubhouse,
Mother and Bucky came looking for us. Mother said
she was anxious to get back home.

Dad had absolutely nothing to say as we drove
home. I tried to make conversation, but all Mom and
Bucky wanted to talk about was horses. Suddenly they
seemed so futile. Why talk about horses, when people
were suffering so?

I went to bed, exhausted, right after dinner. As I lay
there, waiting for sleep to come, I kept wondering
what kind of answer I would get from Dad tomorrow. I
didn't want to get my hopes about the Lower East Side
up too high. And I knew Dad would probably say it
was too dangerous. I also knew that, if God wanted me
to go, He would have to make it possible.

I really searched my heart to see if this was just a do-gooder's scheme to overcome some guilt feelings. Maybe God was opening another door for me, and I wasn't willing to accept it. Strange that the idea of my being president of the company had come up now! Would I be willing to do that, if it were God's will? I could earn a lot of money and support missionaries who could go down into the Lower East Side. They could probably do a lot more good than I could. Was I really afraid that I couldn't make it as president?

I rolled and tossed. Would Dad insist I become president of the company? Would Uncle Alex die in poverty and shame? Would those poor addicts and prostitutes go on living in misery and die a hopeless death, without ever hearing that Jesus could help them?

For me there could be no answer until morning.

4

When morning finally came, I jumped out of bed, got dressed, and was the first one down to breakfast.

Our maid, Cherie, brought my grapefruit. I thought I would wait for my parents.

When Cherie came back with the coffee, I asked her, "Have you seen my folks around? They're late for breakfast."

"I haven't seen a living soul around this place," she responded. "Your folks didn't get up early and go somewhere, did they?"

Could they have pulled a dirty deal on me? Were they afraid to make a decision? Were they afraid to face me? Maybe they figured my religion had gone too far and had decided to deprogram me. Or maybe they had gone to get a psychiatrist.

Cherie poured my coffee. I asked, "Well, have you seen Bucky?"

Cherie laughed. "Bucky? He always sleeps late when he can. He gets mixed-up between breakfast and lunch. When I think he's having lunch, he thinks he's having breakfast."

"Is the car here? Have you seen Harry?"

"Marji, I've never seen you so full of questions. Is something bothering you?"

I stared at my cup. Then I blurted out, "Yes, something is bothering me. I want to know where my parents are!"

"Goodness me, you sound like a little girl. If you are so worried about your parents, why don't you just go and knock on their bedroom door?"

I couldn't do that. I didn't want it to look as if I was so impatient.

Cherie took my half-finished grapefruit and brought my egg. I sort of toyed with it. It tasted horrid, and the coffee had become lukewarm. Food never did much for me when I was nervous.

I couldn't just sit there any longer. I pushed back from the table, stood up, and just then Mom and Dad appeared. I sat back down.

"Good morning, dear," Mother said. "Are you through with breakfast? I guess we got a late start this morning."

She came over to my place and hugged me tight. Then she kissed me on both cheeks. Strange, she usually didn't greet me like that in the morning—at least not until she had had a cup of coffee.

Dad just sort of nodded toward me and didn't say anything. He started right in on his grapefruit. By the time he had finished it, Cherie had his eggs, toast, and coffee in front of him. He ate hungrily and silently. The quiet was killing me.

"Mom, what are you doing today?"

"Oh, just the normal things. I've got a little shopping to do. Why do you ask?"

I was just trying to make conversation, and I was sticking my foot in my mouth. So I decided to get right to the point.

"Did you two have a conversation about me last night?"

Dad jerked his head up. "We don't discuss things like that at mealtime. As soon as we're finished breakfast, we'll go into the library and talk."

Dad went back to his eggs. Mom said nothing.

I wanted to declare that I demanded an answer now—that I was twenty-five years old and resented being treated like a child. But my heart was pounding so heavily that I couldn't have said anything, even if I wanted to. Instead I sat there staring at my half-eaten breakfast and toying with my cup of lukewarm coffee. Finally I pushed back my plate and said, "If it's okay with you, I'll wait in the library."

Dad just nodded.

In the library I eased myself into one of the brown leather chairs and leafed through yesterday's *Wall Street Journal*. An article on the prices of the new fashions caught my eye, but not my attention. Would my future be decided in this room today? What would they tell me? Would Dad insist that I stay in the business? If they did, and if I really was sure God wanted me on the Lower East Side, would it be right for me to defy them? I never had.

It seemed like hours before they finally came in and sat down. Dad broke the silence.

"Marji, your mother and I have thoroughly discussed your idea of going down to the Lower East Side. We want you to know that we are both extremely disappointed and feel you have your head in the clouds."

So far it was exactly what I had expected.

"There are so many dangers on the Lower East Side that it's almost futile to enumerate them," Dad continued. "But let me mention just a few. It has one of the highest crime rates anywhere in the world. That area is infested with junkies, rapists, and perverts. You would be easy prey. And if those people knew you were wealthy, the first thing they would do would be to kidnap you. Then they would probably rape you, and in the end they would kill you."

So that was it. My parents had decided no. And they were trying to paint as dark a picture as possible, and that wasn't too hard when you were talking about the Lower East Side.

"Dad, the way you're describing the Lower East Side is exactly the way I've seen it. I'm sure I don't know all about it, but I've read about it and have visited there."

"You've visited there?" Mom interrupted. "You went down to the Lower East Side without our permission?"

"Marji," Dad demanded, "what were you doing down there?"

Should I spill the beans and tell them I knew all about Uncle Alex? I couldn't without implicating Harry, and I had promised I wouldn't do that.

"Yesterday when I was coming back from Aunt Joyce's, I asked Harry to drive me through the ghetto. I felt as if I needed to see what it was like. Harry just drove through. I was very safe and secure. All I did was look."

Dad breathed a sigh of relief. I figured he was scared to death that somehow I had contacted Uncle Alex.

"Then you're telling me I can't go down there?"

"We didn't say that. After all, you are an adult. We were just trying to warn you about what the Lower East Side is like. We think you ought to be aware of the enormous problems you would face. You might be killed. It's no place for a girl like you. You've got too much potential to throw away your life in a place like that.''

"Dad, I know it's bad. But that's why I have to go there, can't you see? If it were a nice clean place, there wouldn't be people with such enormous needs. I want to go where people are really hurting, where they need to be healed through the love of Jesus.''

"That's another thing we're concerned about," Mom said. "It seems you think this Jesus can solve all the world's problems. Now don't get me wrong. I think Jesus must have been a wonderful person. But a person who lived two thousand years ago can't put food on the table or get people jobs or find them better houses to live in. You've got to get into the real world, Marji. Dream castles are okay for children, but you're twenty-five and all . . . .''

I'd heard that one from her before. People claim that Christians die hungry, beaten, and with all kinds of other problems. And in those moments of great calamity, where is Jesus? He is just a great teacher who had some good ideas.

"Mom, I'm not living in dream castles. I'm not saying that when a person accepts Jesus as Saviour it's like waving a magic wand over him, and all his problems are solved. But when a person receives Jesus, as he learns to trust Him, He is able to help him raise his standard of living. God really *does* answer prayer. You believe that, don't you?''

"Now let's not get into a religious argument," Dad interrupted. "We're discussing your future, Marji. And even though your mother and I disagree about it, we have come to this conclusion: You have our permission to go down to the Lower East Side.''

I couldn't believe my ears! I jumped out of that

leather chair as fast as I had ever moved in my life, ran over, and threw my arms around my dad. Then I ran over and hugged Mom. "Oh, thank you! Thank you!" I was beaming!

"Just a minute, Marji," Dad said sternly. "There are some conditions."

"Conditions?"

"Yes, conditions. We are extremely concerned about your personal safety. So here are the conditions.

"First, you are going to have to stay with your Aunt Joyce. It's safe there."

Safe? I caught myself before I almost blurted out that I nearly got raped going up to her apartment!

"You can go down to the Lower East Side from noon until three each day," Dad continued. "Just three hours. Furthermore, Harry has to be with you at all times. You are to go down and come back in our car. I also plan to hire two bodyguards to look out for your safety."

I couldn't believe it. There would be no way I could reach out to people with those restrictions! If I came down in a chauffeured limousine, how could they expect me to identify with them in their poverty? I could hear them laughing at me already. And two bodyguards? Those guys would have guns, and that would mean there would be no way I could get next to the people who were involved in crime. And from noon until three? There wasn't much action then. The action came at night.

"Dad, are you serious?"

He nodded. "It will have to be that way or not at all. These conditions aren't open to negotiation."

I wanted to blurt out, "Couldn't I stay with Uncle

Alex?'' Somehow I had to bring him into the conversation.

I hit it head-on. ''Isn't there anybody down on the Lower East Side whom I could stay with? Do you have a business friend or a distant relative or something?''

Dad's face turned white as a sheet. Mother's mouth was wide open.

''Is something the matter? You two look as if you've just seen a ghost.'' I laughed.

They obviously didn't think it was funny.

''Okay,'' I said, ''I accept your conditions. But during those three hours I'm down there, I'm going to try to meet every single person on the Lower East Side. It may take me a while, but I'm going to know all about them.''

They looked at each other. I knew what they were thinking: Eventually I would find out about Uncle Alex. Were they willing to risk that? Or would they rather tell me themselves?

''Marji, there is one other thing I have thought of,'' Dad said. ''But I must talk to your mother about it, first.''

It worked!

I excused myself and walked upstairs to my bedroom and waited. This time I was patient. I knew the longer I waited, the greater was the chance for them to tell me about Uncle Alex. Possibly they would find a way for me to go without all those terrible restrictions.

The diamonds on my watch glistened as the sunlight hit them. Then I realized it had already been at least two hours since I left the library!

Finally I heard a gentle knock on my door. When I

opened it, there stood Mom and Dad, with their arms
around each other. They had both been crying.

Mom threw her arms around me, and I started to
cry, too. Then Dad came over and put his arms around
both of us, and he began to sob. Nothing was said. But
I knew what it was; they felt guilt and remorse because
of Uncle Alex.

"Honey," Dad finally said, "we need to talk to you
about something very serious."

He sat down on the edge of my bed and put his head
in his hands. "I guess it's time now for you to know,
Marji, about a terrible tragedy in our family. It's about
your uncle Alex.

"Marji, he isn't in Germany as we told you. He lives
with some woman down on the Lower East Side. I
won't go into all the details of the story; it's still too
painful for me to think about. But it started when your
grandfather Parker's will was read. I was shocked,
amazed, and honestly hurt that he almost cut Alex out
of his will. He gave him only ten percent, and he gave
me the other ninety percent.

"You can't imagine the pressure placed on me after
that. Some of our cousins wrote nasty letters and accused me of scheming to get that ninety percent. I
think your uncle Alex began to believe all the lies
people were telling about me. He reacted violently and
said he would kill me. I had to hire bodyguards for
protection. You can't imagine the fear I lived with."

I began to see there were some parts of the story
Harry didn't know about.

"Uncle Alex began to drink heavily. It wasn't too
long before he was an alcoholic and ended up on the
Lower East Side. I send him five hundred dollars a

month, and he has never contacted me. I know he's getting the money, because he endorses the checks. The president of the bank down there is a friend of mine, and he knows it is Alex who cashes the checks.''

''Marji,'' Mom said, ''you don't know how much it has hurt us to keep this from you. We've been so ashamed of Uncle Alex. Sometimes newspaper reporters try to pick up these stories. It was so embarrassing to your father. Yet we know we were wrong in lying to you.''

She sobbed some more. ''You and Bucky have been such good children to us. We've never known you to cover up anything. Yet here we've covered this up all these years. It's been horrible living with it. We've been trying to forget. Oh, Marji, will you please forgive us?''

I threw my arms around her. ''Of course, Mom. You know I forgive you.''

I felt Dad's hand on my shoulder. He gently pulled me away from Mother and threw his arms around me. ''Honey, does that go for your father, too?''

''Of course, Dad.''

Well, we all stood there crying for I don't know how long. I guess I loved and respected my parents even more after this episode. They weren't Christians, but they were good people. I was so proud of them!

That's when I decided to change my mind. It probably was just a big dream. What could a girl like me do? I had no real experience in counseling. I really didn't even know how to win people to Jesus. Maybe I shouldn't go. Maybe I should just do what Dad wanted and become president of the company. And now that the problem about Uncle Alex was out in the open, maybe our family could come up with some way to really help him.

"Mom and Dad, you're right. I have no business going down to the Lower East Side."

"Oh, no, Marji," Dad said. "Don't say that. We can't get over your love and concern for people who are hurting. I don't know much about Jesus, but I've never seen a more beautiful spirit about something than you've shown us. You didn't demand to do what you wanted to do. You knew we wouldn't understand, and yet you were willing to let us decide. If I ever do become a Christian, I want to be one like you. That love and concern you have for others who are so poor and helpless is what this world needs. If you want to open a counseling center on the Lower East Side, your mother and I will stand behind you one hundred percent. I'll even help pay the rent for the building."

Was I hearing right? Had God performed the miracle I needed? I didn't know. I just threw my arms around my wonderful parents, and we all cried some more.

Finally Mom said, "About those restrictions, Marji. We knew they were unfair. We thought maybe it would stop you. We were wrong in that. So we have another idea."

"Since you know about Uncle Alex now," Dad said, "I think the best thing is to see if you can live with him. I don't know if he'll even consider it. But that spirit of love you're talking about is something that Uncle Alex desperately needs. I just couldn't face the idea of your living down there alone, so I think it would be tremendous if you could live with Uncle Alex. And you'd know firsthand how people live in the ghetto. As I say, I don't know what his situation is, but

I think we should at least explore the possibility.''

What a brilliant idea! And maybe this was one of the reasons why God was giving me such a burden for the Lower East Side. Maybe God would use me to reach out to my uncle Alex. Wouldn't that be something?

"Let me work on it," Dad said. "I'll try to make contact somehow. I can't promise much, but you pray about it."

"Pray about it?" I queried unbelievingly. "Oh, Daddy, do you know what you just said?"

"Oh, my goodness! You've even got *me* thinking that God can help!"

The next few days were ones of great expectancy and excitement. I took time off from work to plan and pray about the venture. I even started to pack. I added that "nice bonus" to my bank account.

But each night, when Dad came home, I met him at the door; and it was always the same. Still no word about Uncle Alex.

Five nights later Dad came bursting through the door. "Marji! Marji! Great news! We made contact!"

"What? How? What did he say? Come on, don't keep me in suspense!"

"Well, I didn't talk to Alex, but my banker friend did, and we have set it up. Alex is living with some woman, but the banker didn't know if it was his wife or not. He thought it best not to ask too many personal questions. But Alex did say he'd be glad to take you in. I have no idea what kind of apartment he lives in, but it will be a roof over your head. And he said he'd watch out for you."

"Oh, praise the Lord!" I said.

"You're to go down next Monday morning. I'll have Harry take you."

"Oh, Dad, I'm so thrilled. But would you let me make one suggestion? Why don't you have Harry take me to the middle of Manhattan? I can take a taxi from there. If I drove up in a chauffeured limousine, I can just imagine the response from the people. They really stared at us when we drove through the other day. Besides, I don't think it would be a good idea for people to know I'm a rich kid. Remember about kidnapping?"

Dad got very serious. "I guess you're right again, honey. It would be taking a risk to have Harry drive you down there. Yes, your idea of the taxi is the best way to go."

Now all I had to do was wait until Monday. But with all the excitement, I still felt nervous. What would it be like to live on the Lower East Side? Would I be mugged or raped or maybe killed? What about the rats? Oh, how I hated them! and the roaches! Maybe Uncle Alex's place wouldn't even be clean. Maybe his woman was an alcoholic, too. Could I live in filth?

Dear Lord, I prayed, *give me strength to face whatever is ahead.*

"I guess I could do that."

"Of course you can. And you've learned something today. Now you know how to talk to God!"

Harry grinned. Then he turned abruptly, got into the limousine, and drove off.

Before I had a chance to feel alone, I saw a taxi coming and hailed it. The driver merely pulled up to the curb—didn't even offer to help me with my suitcases. I stuffed them into the backseat as best I could, then I climbed in.

"Where to, lady?"

"The Lower East Side. The address is one-eleven East Ninth Street."

He turned and gawked at me. "Where did you say?"

"I said one-eleven East Ninth Street."

"That's what I thought you said. I mean, lady, that's a really nasty neighborhood!"

Apparently everybody was afraid of the Lower East Side.

"Lady, you from out of town or something?"

I didn't want to tell him about myself. I certainly couldn't tell him I was a rich kid coming down to try to save the Lower East Side. He would have dropped me off at Bellevue Psychiatric Hospital.

When I didn't respond, he didn't say any more. We finally got down to East Ninth Street. I found it hard to believe what I was seeing: burned-out tenements, garbage overflowing the streets and sidewalks, ransacked cars, graffiti all over the walls.

It was difficult to tell the tenement numbers. In fact, there didn't seem to be many. Finally the driver pulled over to the curb.

"Okay, lady, this is the end of the line."

I opened the door, since I didn't figure he'd get out to help me with my suitcases.

"That'll be fifteen dollars, lady."

"Fifteen dollars?" I exploded. "Your meter says five dollars."

"Oh, did I forget to mention that I have to charge extra for your suitcases? Six suitcases is like taking three more people. I'm really giving you a bargain!" His voice was dripping with sarcasm.

"Besides, lady, I have to charge extra for coming into the Lower East Side. You know, like a war zone." And he laughed.

I didn't think it was at all funny, and his arrogance was really getting to me. I'd ridden in taxis many times before, and I knew that occasionally you find a turkey like this one. I wasn't about to pay him more than the meter showed.

"Listen, mister," I said. "You can't pull a fast one on me. I know New York City about as well as you do. My dad works here, and I know my way around. There is no way you're going to charge me extra. You're trying to rip me off!"

He hoisted his fat frame around to face me. Pointing his finger right at my nose, he shouted, "Listen, you little twerp. Don't you get sassy with me. If you think I'm trying to rip you off, why don't you just go over there and call the cops? We'll let them settle this. I don't know what your game is, but it's fifteen dollars, or else!"

What a jam. I knew it was time someone stood up to these turkeys. But I really wasn't in much of a position to do it.

"Okay, mister. I still don't believe your story, but here's ten dollars. That's it!"

I dropped the bill on the seat beside him. He crumpled it up and threw it back at me. "Listen, lady, like I said, it's fifteen bucks. If you don't like it, call the cops. And if you don't pay me right now, I'm going to have to start charging you waiting time. In two minutes the price goes up to twenty bucks."

I knew what he was driving at. He was really hoping I would get out and call the cops. Then he would take off with my six suitcases! I had paid several hundred dollars just for the suitcases, not counting all the valuable things I had inside them. He knew those suitcases were valuable, and he wanted to rip me off. So I decided I'd better pay.

I pulled out a five, added it to the crumpled ten, and handed it to him. "Okay, mister, you win this time. But I want to tell you something. I'm a Christian, and God's going to get you for what you've done!"

He roared with laughter. "Well, I don't know what a Christian is supposed to be. I thought they were holy. Do they all yell like you?"

I guess for the first time I realized how furious I had become. I was nervous about coming down here, anyway—and then this on top of it. Maybe I shouldn't have yelled. Maybe God wouldn't get him, after all.

I pulled my suitcases out of the seat and stacked them on the curb. As I pulled the last one out and slammed the door, he took off so fast his tires screeched. He was nervous about being down here, too!

Still angry about being ripped off and angrier at myself for being angry, I turned to look for 111. Which tenement was it? I couldn't see any numbers at all. How was I to know which one to go to?

What a predicament. I couldn't leave my six suitcases on the curb while I went knocking on doors. And how could I find the right address?

I saw a girl standing on the corner a few feet away. Funny, I hadn't noticed her before. Just then a man walked by, and I heard her mumble, "Wanna have a good time?"

So that was it. She was a prostitute.

The man walked by. Maybe it was too early in the day.

She probably knew where 111 was!

"Hey, miss, could you tell me where one-eleven East Ninth Street is?"

She sauntered over and stood in front of me. "Sure! It's down at the end of the block. See down there on the right-hand side? The last building on the corner—that's one-hundred and eleven."

"Oh, thanks," I responded. "That taxi driver let me out at the wrong place. Thanks."

You should have seen me struggle to pick up six suitcases! It would have made a great comedy!

No way—finally I was able to get the four smaller ones, one in each hand and one under each arm. But the other two were too heavy and too bulky. Why hadn't I thought of that?

I turned around, but the girl had walked off. What was I going to do?

I had to take my chances. I would run down to 111 as fast as I could with the four suitcases. I would get them inside the door and then run back here for the other two.

I tightened my grip on the four and took off. A voice behind me yelled, "Hey, lady, you forgot two of your suitcases!"

I stopped and turned around. It was the same girl.

"Yes, I know," I yelled back. "I'm just going to run down to one-eleven and put these inside the door, and then I'll run back."

"You can't do that, lady. By the time you turn around, these two suitcases will be gone."

I walked back toward her. "Could you do me a favor? Could you guard those two for me while I'm gone, please? I'll only be a minute."

"Sure! Why not?"

"That's awfully nice of you. I do appreciate it."

"No problem. No problem."

That wasn't too hard. People seemed to be nicer here than some other parts of the city.

I grabbed the four smaller suitcases again and walked as quickly as I could to 111. I tried the doorknob—locked.

Now what was I going to do? If I left these suitcases on the steps and ran back after the other two, would they be here when I got back? I needed another guard.

I glanced up to where the girl was standing with my two bigger suitcases. She wasn't there. Neither were the suitcases!

I don't swear, but I felt like it then. First that taxi driver had ripped me off—now that girl. I was becoming more irritated by the moment. All these lost souls didn't seem quite so attractive now! Didn't they realize I was here to help them? I was just about ready to quit right then!

I grabbed the door handle and twisted—nothing. So I banged on the door.

I heard steps coming. I was about to meet my uncle Alex! The door opened, and I stared into the eyes of a young man, obviously not Uncle Alex.

"Hello there," I said. "I'm looking for Alex Parker's apartment."

"Oh, yeah, we heard you were coming. We're all waiting for you."

That seemed strange. A welcome party, maybe?

"Mister, could you do me a favor? Could I put these suitcases inside the door? I've got to go back to that corner. I left two suitcases there, and they're gone. But I think I know who has them."

"Just put them inside the door. I'll guard them for you."

"Oh, no you don't," I said. "I just went through that 'guard' business with that girl. She's supposed to be guarding them, and they're gone!"

"Come on, you can trust me. We people in this tenement stick together. We guard each other's apartments. And since you're Alex's niece, I have a responsibility to guard you. Get it?"

I really didn't have much choice. I had to hurry to try to get those other suitcases back.

"Okay, I trust you. But if I come back and those four suitcases are gone, believe me there's going to be blood all over this street!"

He laughed. "Alex didn't warn me about how vicious you are. I thought you were supposed to be a good little girl."

I felt so embarrassed. I guessed I had better cool it and project a better image. I really hadn't been acting like a Christian.

I turned and ran down the street. Halfway up the block was a burned-out tenement with no doors or windows. I hurried up the steps and peered inside. At the end of the hall was the girl, opening my suitcases.

I jumped inside and yelled, "Lady, can't anybody trust anybody around here? Why did you steal my suitcases?"

She already had my coat out and was putting it on. I ran toward her, absolutely furious. I grabbed the coat and started to jerk it off her. She jerked back.

"Calm down, sister," she said. "Let's make a deal. I give you the suitcases, and I keep the coat. Okay?"

Everybody was making deals: taxicab drivers, prostitutes, who else?

"A deal? You've got to be kidding. I want my suitcases, and I want my coat, too."

"Hey, lady, we have our own laws down here. Why don't you just call the police? And if you do, I'm going to file charges against you that you tried to steal my coat."

I had had enough of this nonsense and decided to call her bluff. That's exactly what I would do: call the police.

As I started away, she yelled, "Lady, don't forget you'll get six months in the slammer for stealing somebody's coat!"

I stopped short. It wasn't what she said. It was my stupid attitude. If I called the cops on this girl, how would I ever be able to reach people like her? A friend of the cops would be an enemy to them. All I needed to do was to create a big scene on my first day, and that would be the end of my mission. I felt so embarrassed about the way I had acted. Yes, I'd better go back and try to work a deal with this girl.

I slowly walked back to her. "Okay," I said, "you got your deal. You can have the coat. I'll take the suitcases."

I reached for the handles. "Oh, by the way, what is your name?"

For the first time I saw her smile. "You can call me Patsy."

"Well, glad to meet you, Patsy. My name is Marji. Marji Parker."

"That's a nice name," she said. "And if you don't mind my asking, what's a nice girl like you doing down here? You must be stupid, crazy, or out of your mind."

Should I tell her I was down here to try to win people to Jesus? I had blown it with the cab driver and had almost blown it with this prostitute. So I just gave a flippant answer. "Oh, I'm just kind of checking the place out."

Patsy jumped back. "Don't tell me you're an under-cover cop?"

That struck me funny. "Oh, Patsy, I wouldn't have the first idea about how to shoot a gun or arrest some-body."

"Well, then, what are you?"

"I guess you just might call me a Christian."

"A Christian? You're a Christian, and you tell me you have just come to check this place out?"

"I guess so." I didn't know how else to explain my being here.

"Well, Marji, lotsa luck. I thought Christians went to those nice churches uptown."

And with that she slipped my coat off and handed it

to me. "Here, take it," she said. "I decided I don't really want it."

"Well, thank you," I said. "Things are looking up."

Patsy glowered at me. I knew she really wanted the coat, but I also knew I needed it. I stuffed it into the suitcase, walked away from Patsy and the burned-out tenement, and over to 111.

I started wondering about the other four suitcases. Would that young man still be guarding them? I bounded up the steps and tried the door—locked. I kicked it again. Just then it opened. There stood the young man, smiling. And there sat my four suitcases. Maybe things would turn out all right, after all.

"Hey, thanks for watching these for me."

"Like I tell you, lady, we look out for each other. Don't you forget it."

"I won't. Can you tell me which apartment my uncle lives in?"

"Yeah, he's in two-fourteen. Let me help you up the stairs."

He carried the four, and I took the two and followed him. The hall was filthy, with graffiti all over the walls. Someone had used it for a bathroom, and the smell nauseated me.

When we came to 214, I knocked. A moment later the door flew open. There stood my uncle Alex.

I couldn't believe my eyes. To call this person standing before me my uncle was going to be one of the most difficult things I had ever had to do. I just couldn't believe my eyes!

6

Could this really be Uncle Alex? He looked like something out of a horror movie. Two of his front teeth were missing. When he smiled, I could see that the rest of his teeth were filthy dirty. His breath almost knocked me over. He needed a shave. What little hair he had left was dirty and unkempt. And his stomach pouched out over his belt.

His pants were several sizes too large and looked as if they had never seen a cleaner. His undershirt was soiled and ripped. His tennis shoes were filthy. I noticed a dirty toe sticking through the end of one.

Could this be my father's brother—my father, who was so immaculate about his appearance?

I guess I must have been standing there with my mouth open. Uncle Alex broke the silence. "Well, come on in, kid. I understand that you're coming down here to change this world." Then he cackled.

I didn't react to what he was saying. I was still so shocked by his appearance. And as I walked into the room, I had some more culture shock. The place was filthy. I'd read about tenement houses and their filth. But reading about it and seeing it—and knowing I was going to have to live in it—were different things!

I tried not to contrast it to my beautiful home in Long Island, but I couldn't help it. I'd never been in a house or apartment with garbage strewn all over the place. The broken furniture, what little there was of it, looked like rejects from a secondhand store—stuff they would throw away. And the sink was piled high with what I judged must have been at least a week's worth of dirty dishes. How could anyone ever live in a place like this?

My first reaction was to turn around and walk out. Then I could hear what everyone would say: "Uh-huh! Just another do-gooder. She couldn't stomach it."

Oh, no!! If this was a way of discouraging me, it was going to take a lot more than that. I was here on a mission. I believed God had sent me. And I was going to stay!

Just then, a middle-aged woman walked out of the bedroom. She smiled, and I noticed that she had all her teeth. Her dress was very plain, but it was clean. In fact, she wasn't too bad-looking. Was she Uncle Alex's girl friend or his wife?

"I've been so excited about you coming," she said. "I'm glad that you've come down here to try to help us."

Well, this was a change. At least she seemed appreciative. I liked her immediately.

"Okay, kid, you can see we don't have much here," Alex said. "It's the best we got. You're welcome, if you want to stay."

"Thanks, Uncle. I just can't tell you how much I appreciate you folks opening your home to me. I know it's quite an imposition."

Alex laughed. "Listen, I know this ain't the beautiful home you're used to. But one thing you've got to understand, kid; it won't be long until you see that there are other people living on this earth besides rich people. There's a bunch of us down here on the Lower

East Side. We're human, too—whether you like it or not."

So Uncle Alex was still bitter. And now he was starting to pour it on me. I would have none of it.

"Let's get one thing straight from the first, Uncle Alex. I don't think it's necessary for us to carry past problems into what I'm trying to do down here. I know what's happened, and I have great sympathy for you. My father has grieved many years over your plight; but there's not much I can do about it, at least not now. I know my dad is sending you five hundred dollars a month and . . . ."

When I mentioned the money, Alex exploded. "Listen here, you little snirp, if you don't change your attitude, I'll throw you out on the street, suitcases and all. You'll be sleeping on a park bench. There's no way I take charity, and I want you to know it. I'm my own man, and I do what I want. That measly five hundred bucks your father sends me is peanuts to him. Besides, I should have gotten a whole lot more. It's really my money, anyway. If your old man put you up to this, you can tell him he's lucky to only have to send five hundred dollars a month!"

He had moved so close that his finger was almost touching my nose.

"I've heard about do-gooders like you before, kid. All kinds of them come around here. But they don't last long. And you won't either. Mark my words.

"But let me tell you one thing. As long as you're here, I'll look out for you. You're still my niece, and nobody's going to rap you on the side of the head, if I can help it. I got friends out there on the street, and the word is out not to lay a hand on you. Understand that?"

I'd almost blown it again! I'd known I shouldn't have mentioned that money. I guess it made it look as if the only reason he was helping me was because of the money. He sure straightened me out on that! I had to think of something quickly.

"Uncle Alex, would you please forgive me for mentioning that money? I didn't use common sense, and I should have had more sympathy and respect for you. Please forgive me. I'll never mention it again."

He sort of shrugged, so I decided I'd better change the subject.

"Uncle Alex, you didn't introduce me to this attractive lady here."

He smiled. Good! "I'm sorry, Marji. I guess you've never met her before. This is my wife, Amilda. Amilda, this is my niece Marji."

Amilda came over and gave me a friendly hug. "You're so attractive, Marji. I knew you were coming, but I didn't expect a beautiful young girl like you."

That made me like her even more. She was such a warm person. How she could ever live with my Uncle Alex, I'll never know.

Alex didn't lift a finger toward my suitcases, but Amilda helped me to carry them into my bedroom. There was a small cot over to one side. Otherwise only a bunch of old boxes cluttered the tiny room. But it was a place to stay.

They prepared a meal for me, and it wasn't too bad. Amilda did know how to cook, and I was hungry. I offered to do the dishes, but Amilda insisted that she do them, since, as she put it, she "hadn't had time to do them all day." Anyway, I dried them, and we got better acquainted as we talked.

Thanks, God, for Amilda.

Uncle Alex sat around watching TV and drinking beer, while we did the dishes. Amilda said that was about all he ever did. I wondered what could happen to a man's self-respect to make him end up like that.

That night I could hardly sleep. Every so often a siren roared through the streets. And people were yelling. And loud jazz blared from the tenement next door; they must have been having a party or something. It wasn't at all like the quiet of home. Would I ever get used to it?

No one was around when I got up the next morning. Cherie wasn't here to fix breakfast. I snooped around until I found some cold cereal and milk. That was breakfast.

I had no idea when Uncle Alex and Aunt Amilda would be getting up. After all, what did they have to get up for? In fact, what did they have to live for?

Back in my bedroom, I had my devotions. I must confess that I was still rather scared about my mission. I didn't know what to do next. I knew it was a matter of trusting God. As I memorized some Scripture, God seemed so real. I could sense His presence. Yes, God was indeed in the ghetto!

When Aunt Joyce had heard what I was hoping to do, she had purchased John Benton's other books and sent them to me. Now I pulled them out of my suitcase.

I knew that he and his wife, Elsie, had a home for girls up in Garrison and had had years of experience working with drug addicts and prostitutes. I made a mental note to get in touch with them as soon as possible, to learn how to help these girls. In the meantime, perhaps reading his books would help me better understand some of the problems the girls faced.

I pulled out one titled *Suzie* and read most of the morning, until I finally heard Alex and Amilda in the other room. I went out to tell them good morning, although it was nearly noon.

Amilda smiled, but Alex just grunted. He was going to be a hard nut to crack.

That afternoon I went out on the street to look for a small storefront for my counseling center.

As I walked down the street, who should be standing on that same corner but Patsy. I decided to say hi. But as I got closer, the first thing I noticed was her black eye. It was a terrible mess.

"Oh, my," I said. "What in the world happened to you?"

She ignored me.

I tried again. "Did your husband beat you up?"

"Listen, I don't have no husband. This black eye I got from a trick. You know what that is?"

I nodded.

"Well, I propositioned a sharp one; and when we got to the hotel, of course I got his money first. But as soon as we crawled out of the bed, he grabbed me by the throat and threw me on the floor. I started to scream and kicked him. He doubled over and started howling. That's when I leaped for the door. But as I did, he grabbed me backwards, doubled up his fist, and hit me in the eye, just as hard as he could.

"When I woke up, I was on the floor, and he wasn't

around anywhere. Oh, the pain was so bad! And the money was gone! That guy got what he wanted; all I got was this horrible black eye. So help me, if I see that one around again, I'll kill him!''

From what I'd read, I knew prostitution was dangerous. Every so often I'd seen in the papers that some pervert had killed a prostitute and cut her up into little pieces or stuffed her into a plastic bag or even thrown her from a rooftop. I guess Patsy was lucky she only had a black eye! Oh, if somehow I could help her get out of prostitution.

"Listen, Patsy," I sympathized. "Why don't you come over to my apartment? I'll put some cold cloths on your eye. That will bring down the swelling and ease the pain. Besides, with you looking like that, no guy will want your services." I laughed.

"Hey, listen! That's not funny. Some of these old guys are so perverted that they would want me just because I had a black eye! It's sick! But they'll pay."

"Well, Patsy, I know of something that would do more for you than a cold cloth for your eye."

She looked at me unbelievingly. "What's that?"

"If you'd just give your life over to Jesus Christ, He'd give you peace and love and everything you'll ever need."

"Aw, nuts! I thought you had a *real* answer. Don't try to give me no religion or nothing like that. Like I told you yesterday, that's okay for uptown, but not here."

"Patsy, I'm not talking about religion. I'm talking about a way of life. If you'd just turn your life over to Jesus, you'd never be sorry."

She stepped forward; her face was about three

inches from mine. "Listen, girl, why don't you get lost? I've got to make some money. If I don't, my pimp is going to black my other eye. Then I won't be able to see nothin'. Or maybe he'll break my arm or my leg. So get lost before you get me into big trouble."

I stepped back. "Listen, you're going to get hungry. Why can't we have lunch together?"

"I said to get out of here!" Patsy screamed.

"Isn't there something I can do for you?"

She got close to my face again and screamed at the top of her voice: "Yeah, *get lost!*" Then she stomped off.

As she moved away from me, I breathed a quick prayer: *Lord, isn't there some way I can reach Patsy? Please, God, would You tell me how I can reach her for You?*

Like a flash the answer came—a deep impression in my mind: "Give her your coat."

"But, God, that's the only good coat I have. It cost a lot of money, and I'm going to need it down here. Maybe I could buy her a used one."

I argued with God that way, but I knew what the answer was. I had to give Patsy *that* coat, not some other one.

Back at the apartment I pulled the coat from my suitcase and went looking for Patsy. She wasn't hard to find; she was always on the same corner.

I walked up and shoved the coat into her arms. "Here, take this."

Startled, she stepped back. "Why you giving this to me?"

"It's my way and God's way of letting you know we really do care about you."

She softened. Then she lovingly put the coat on and began to strut back and forth. "Beautiful! Just beautiful!" She stroked the sleeves. "This coat cost a lot of money, didn't it? Where'd you get that kind of money?"

"Oh, I just had it."

"What do you mean, you just had it? Was a good little girl like you soliciting johns? I'll bet with your looks you can really rake in the money in one night, can't you?"

I couldn't tell her my dad had bought it for me; she would start asking too many questions. I didn't want anyone to know I came from a wealthy family.

When I didn't answer, Patsy suddenly jerked the coat off and let it drop on the filthy sidewalk.

"What are you doing, Patsy?"

"I know your game! You're tryin' to buy me!"

"No! No! I just wanted you to have this coat. That's all!"

"Listen, nobody ever treated me like that. Nobody gives away a good coat like that. Whatever you're up to, I'm not going to go along with it!"

"Please believe me, Patsy. I have nothing in mind except to give you the coat. It's going to get cold or wet out here one of these evenings, and you're likely to catch pneumonia and die. I wouldn't want that to happen. I've got no angle but to give you my coat."

Patsy stepped back and squinted at me. "Everybody's got an angle," she said. "You got to get wise to the streets. The street says if I take this coat, I owe you something. It's like my pimp. He gave me a beautiful apartment and a poodle. I thought everything was fine, until one day he pushed me out the door and onto the street. Then he said, 'Baby, this it it. Now you got to work.' Dumb me, if I had refused his gifts, I might be working on my own instead of for him.''

"Listen, Patsy, that's not the way it is with me. There is absolutely no obligation.''

"I don't believe you. Nobody gives a good coat to a stranger.''

I started to walk away. "Do what you want with the coat,'' I said over my shoulder. "I can see that only God can convince you that I really care about you.''

When I got to the middle of the block, I sneaked a quick glance back. Patsy was putting the coat on.

I just continued walking away. Then I heard some-one running behind me. I turned. It was Patsy.

"Tell me honestly,'' she said as she came up beside me. "Why did you give me your coat?''

"It was God's love that helped me do it. That's all.''

She stroked the sleeves of the coat again and brushed some of the dirt off. As she walked away, I heard her mumble, "I need that kind of love.''

"Wait, Patsy!'' I called after her. "If you have a minute, let me tell you about God's love. Do you have just one minute?''

"Yeah, I guess I got a minute.''

I pulled my New Testament from my purse and began to show Patsy that, as a sinner, she needed to ask Jesus to forgive her for her sins and to receive Him as her personal Saviour. She hung on every word.

She seemed to be following so closely that I asked, "Patsy, would you like to receive Jesus as your Saviour?''

"Marji, you're a wonderful girl. I can't get over this coat. But I can't make that decision now.

I need more time."

"That's what everybody wants, Patsy—more time.
But we don't know when our time will be up. Right
now is the time to give your life to Jesus."

"I got to think about it, Marji. I just have to."

Just then another girl walked by. She, too, was scan-
tily dressed. Patsy grabbed her arm. "Carmen, come
on. I got something for you!"

She introduced us. Carmen was skinny and looked
cold. I wondered if this was the Carmen the boy on the
rooftop at Aunt Joyce's had told me about. But there
was no way I could ask. Besides, Patsy's next question
threw me.

"Marji, have you got another coat?"

I started to laugh, but Patsy was serious. "No, I
don't have one right now, but I'll sure try to get
another one. I guess I should have brought a whole
truckload of coats, shouldn't I?"

Patsy and I laughed, but Carmen just stared at us.
She had no idea what this coat business was all about.

I had just started to explain when a big, expensive
car pulled to the curb and a well-dressed guy got out. I
remember wondering what someone like this was
doing down here on the Lower East Side. But when
Patsy and Carmen saw him, they took off, running at
top speed. I almost did, but really didn't know of any
reason why I should. So I stood my ground.

"Hey, what's goin' on here?" the big guy asked as
he walked up to me. "Don't you know who those two
girls are?"

"Sure, I know them. They're Patsy and Carmen.
They're drug addicts and prostitutes."

"They are *what?*" he asked incredulously.

I repeated it.

Before I knew what had happened, he had grabbed my blouse at the collar and twisted, pulling me up close as he did. "Listen, sister, I don't know who you are or what your game is. But there's one thing you and me got to get straight. Don't you ever call my girls prostitutes and drug addicts. Those are dirty words, and if I hear them from you again, I'm going to slap you good! You understand?"

Uh-oh! He must be the girls' pimp, making his money off their earnings. I'd heard about pimps, and I knew they were mean.

I grabbed his hands in mine, trying to pull them from my blouse. No use. "Listen, mister, I'm sorry. I was just trying to tell these girls about Jesus—how He wants to save them and help them."

I felt his hand come down hard on my face, and I tasted the blood oozing from my lip. I tried to scream, but his hand tightened around my throat, shutting off my voice.

"My girls don't need no Jesus, or anybody else, to help them. I take care of them!"

My heart was pounding wildly. I knew pimps were killers. Now I had messed with his girls, and he was going to make me pay for it.

Behind me a loud voice ordered, "Hey, what's going on here? Drop your hands from that girl!"

The pimp reluctantly obeyed. I turned, and there stood a cop. Was I ever glad to see him!

"Okay, you two. What gives? Is this guy trying to get you out onto the street, lady?"

I started to blurt out that this pimp had slapped me

and threatened me. I really wanted to have him arrested. But I knew that if I ever did that, he would really be out to kill me. Besides that, then I might never be able to reach Patsy and Carmen.

I decided to play it cool.

"It's okay, officer. We were having a little discussion, and I got out of line."

I turned to the pimp. "Sir, I'm sorry for opening my big mouth. Would you forgive me?"

His mouth dropped open, but he knew he had to go along with the game. "Sure, sure! Yeah, no problem whatever."

"Listen, young lady, you sure you're not in trouble?" the cop insisted. "Was Benny trying to force you to work for him? That lip looks bad!"

I didn't want to lie. But neither did I want to get anybody in trouble. I had to reach these people. I had to live among them. "Officer, I assure you there's no problem."

"Okay, if you say so. I haven't seen you around before. Maybe you don't know this guy is Benny Barnes. He's one of the most notorious pimps around the block. He's got a stable of girls working for him, and he's always looking for more. I really don't believe your story, but there's nothing I can do to arrest him. Let me give you some advice, though. You stay away from this turkey, or you're going to get into serious trouble."

I glanced at Benny. Yes, he did look mean. It was the first time I had met a pimp, and I hoped it would be the last.

"Yes, officer, I know what you're saying. But I have no problem with Benny."

"Well, if you have any problem, you let me know.

I'm just itching to bust him. And when I do, I want to bust him good!''

Benny sneered. "Listen, Galigan, you heard what the gal said. I'm clean. You ain't got nothin' on me!"

"All right," the officer answered. "But I'm going to walk back to the corner, and I'm going to watch you two. If I see any more violence, you're going to get it, Benny. You understand?"

Benny just spit on the ground.

When the officer got out of earshot, I turned to Benny and said, "Whew! That was close!"

"What do ya mean, close? Cops don't make any difference. They just act tough."

"Okay, Benny, have it your way. But believe me, I wasn't trying to do any harm to Patsy and Carmen."

He pointed his finger at my face. "Listen, sister, I'm givin' you just this one warning. The next time I catch you talkin' to those girls, I'm going to stomp you good. That cop won't always be around! There's a couple of girls who don't mess with me no more. You know what I mean?"

I had a good idea what he meant.

Benny walked back to his car. As he opened the door to get in, he pointed his finger at me again. "Just one more time, baby, and it's all over for you. You hear me?"

I heard him!

How was I going to reach Patsy and Carmen now? The answer had seemed so simple: just start talking to them about Jesus. But that was before Benny entered the picture. Now it wouldn't be safe for them to talk to me. It wouldn't be safe for me to talk to them, either. Would Benny carry out his threat? Suddenly I didn't feel very brave!

7

The pimpmobile burned rubber as Benny took off. I stood there, stunned. My lip was beginning to swell, and I figured I'd better go put some cold packs on it. I hoped the cut wasn't so deep that I'd have to have stitches. That could lead to a lot of questions I didn't want to answer just now.

As I turned and started toward Uncle Alex's apartment, I heard footsteps behind me. A man's voice yelled: "Hey, lady. Wait a minute!"

Oh, no! Not more trouble. I hardly dared look. But when I glanced over my shoulder, I recognized the cop.

Relieved, I stopped and waited for him. "Hey, thanks for helping me out of that little jam, officer."

"I just wanted to check again," he said. "I wanted to be sure Benny wasn't trying to force you out onto the street."

This cop sure was persistent. He must really want to get something on Benny. But there was no way I was going to turn him in.

"Now listen, young lady, I've got to tell you something. I don't know what you're doing down here. You look like a person who doesn't belong on the Lower East Side. But I got to tell you about that pimp. He's bad news. Nobody messes with Benny, and he really treats his girls mean."

The officer lowered his voice to a confidential tone.

"We can't prove it yet, but we think he's already killed five girls. So you stay away from him!"

I nodded. What would have happened if that officer hadn't been there? What would I have done if Benny had forced me into his pimpmobile? That probably would have been the last anyone would have seen or heard of me. Maybe I was wrong in coming here.

Then I remembered Patsy and Carmen. They really needed Jesus. And what about this cop? Maybe he needed to know Jesus, too.

"Sir, let me tell you why I'm down here. I want to help these people, to give them something to live for. Now I don't want you to think I'm a religious nut, but I have something I want to share with these people: I want to tell them that Jesus loves them. In fact, His love for them was so great that He died for them. Now He wants to change their lives."

The officer's mouth flew open. "What do you mean, you're not a religious nut? Anybody who tries to help these people has got to be some kind of nut. Don't you know these people can't be helped? The government has wasted billions of dollars trying to help these cases, and nothing has worked. We have all sorts of federal programs and state programs and city programs. We rehabilitated these tenements. We swept the streets. We gave them jobs. I mean *nothing* helps!"

"Sir, I know it looks that way. But has anyone really made an honest attempt to give them Jesus?"

"Give them Jesus?"

"Yes, Jesus. It won't take millions of dollars. It'll just take someone to show them that Jesus really loves them. Believe me, there'll be a great turnaround in their lives when they take Jesus as their Saviour."

"Well, maybe you got a point. I really don't know."

I took the cue. "What about you?" I asked. "Have you received Jesus as your Saviour?"

"Now wait a minute! I don't need religion. My wife's got enough for both of us. All I'm telling you is to stay away from Benny Barnes, or some preacher will be preaching a farewell sermon—over *your* casket!"

He turned and strode away.

Back at the apartment, Uncle Alex sat—fat, dirty, drinking a beer, and watching a soap opera. I thought I could sneak by and into the bathroom, but just then a commercial came on, and he looked my way.

"Hey, what in the world happened to you?" he asked when he saw my lip.

"Nothing really. Just a little scratch."

He laughed. "Don't tell me you met up with your first mugger? or a gang? Or did you slip on some garbage?"

"No, nothing like that. Just some guy slapped me."

That brought him to the edge of his chair. "Somebody slapped you? Hey, wait a minute! The word's out on the street not to touch you. Nobody slaps my niece and gets by with it. You tell me who did it, and I'll go out and rap him. Nobody touches my niece!"

That was a change. At least he was willing to defend me!

"What was his name?" he demanded.

"Oh, the turkey's a pimp. Benny Barnes."

Uncle Alex flew out of his chair. "Benny Barnes?" he screamed. "Did you say Benny Barnes?"

"Yes, Benny Barnes."

"Oh, no, Marji! It would have been better if you had tangled with the wildest lion in Africa. Benny Barnes just has to be the meanest guy down here on the Lower East Side."

"That's what I hear."

"Nobody messes with Benny," Uncle Alex warned. "He'll do you in quicker than you can blink your eyes. They tell me he has five notches on his switchblade from knocking off five girls."

"That's what the cop said, too."

"The cops? Oh, no! Don't tell me you called the cops, Marji! You just don't do that around here. Especially, you don't call the cops on Benny Barnes. Oh, you stupid little girl. You did the wrong thing. I mean the *wrong* thing. You have got to pack your bags and get out of here right now, or Benny Barnes is going to come looking for you. You can't call the cops on him!"

Uncle Alex headed for my room and started throwing my things into the suitcases.

"Wait! Wait a minute, Uncle Alex! It wasn't like that at all! Benny slapped me because I was talking to two of his girls. The cop came up. I didn't call him. But I covered for Benny. I told the cop it wasn't anything. I know I can't call the cops on these people if I want to help them. So just stay cool. I think everything is going to be all right."

"Well, let's hope so," Alex said as he retreated back to face his TV. "But if you ever see Benny coming, you run and scream with all your might!"

I thought Uncle Alex must have been exaggerating. If Benny had wanted to, he could have stabbed me, instead of slapping me. But maybe it was because my guardian angels wouldn't let him go any farther. Let's hope so.

"You better take care of that lip," Alex said.

I walked into the bathroom and peered into the grimy mirror. My lip was badly cut! With a cold washcloth, I wiped off the blood. At least it had stopped bleeding. I wouldn't need stitches.

As I walked back into the living room, Aunt Amilda walked in. She took one look at my lip and screamed, "Alex, you good-for-nothing, dirty, filthy bum. Whatever made you slap Marji?"

Alex bounded out of his chair. "What?" he yelled. "What did you say?"

"Just look at that poor child, you stupid jerk! Why did you slap her?"

"No! No! It wasn't Uncle Alex, Aunt Amilda. He wouldn't do a thing like that!"

"Are you kidding? He's slapped me around, especially when he's had too much to drink."

Alex looked so embarrassed. I knew I'd better come to his rescue. So I walked over and put my arms around him. "Now, now, Aunt Amilda, don't be too hard on him. He promised to look out for me. Didn't you, Uncle Alex?"

I could tell by his half-embarrassed grin that he was enjoying someone making a fuss over him.

"That's right, Amilda. I'm going to look out for my little niece. She's a good girl—smart, too."

I threw my arms around him, squeezed him tight, and kissed his cheek—whiskers, dirt, and all. By now he was really grinning!

Aunt Amilda came over to examine my lip more closely. "Okay, what really happened?"

"It was Benny Barnes," Uncle Alex explained.

Amilda turned white. "No! No! No! Not Benny Barnes!"

I nodded.

"Oh, girl, you're lucky to be alive. Right now you might be tied up in some room, and then he'd be putting you out on the street as a prostitute. You're really lucky!"

"No, I wouldn't say *lucky*, Aunt Amilda," I said. "I'd say it was my guardian angel."

Uncle Alex laughed. "That's a good one! I'm sure guardian angels aren't stupid. No guardian angel would ever come to the Lower East Side!"

We all laughed.

"Listen, I'm okay now," I assured them. "I've got to get out there and look for a storefront for my counseling center. I don't think Benny will be around for a while. He took off when that cop came by."

"Counseling center?" Aunt Amilda asked. "Is that what you intend to do?"

"Well, it will be more than just counseling. I want a place for people to come in off the street, a place where I can give them some encouragement and hope in this life. It won't be a social agency; it'll just be a place where people can come in and talk about their problems and where I can talk to them about Jesus. I guess you might call it an evangelistic center."

"Like a mission?" Alex asked.

"Not exactly. I don't plan to serve meals or preach or anything like that. I just want a place where I can talk to people."

"I think the first person you ought to get in there is Benny Barnes," Uncle Alex said. "Wouldn't that be something if he got religion?" Alex laughed at that idea.

"That may not be so funny, Uncle Alex. There have been some tremendous conversions. You name it: murderers, gangsters, addicts, alcoholics, prostitutes, and even pimps. God can convert anyone!"

"He's never run into Benny Barnes!" he said, still laughing.

I looked my uncle straight in the eye. "You'd better be careful. God is after *you!*"

It was as if someone had taken a wet rag and wiped the smile off his face! He stared at the floor and mumbled, "It's too late. I don't think God would have any use for the likes of me."

"Don't say that! God loves everyone. I'm not sorry that I received Him. Uncle Alex, you need Him, too."

"Marji, it seems all right for the likes of you. But not for me. You don't know much about me."

"That doesn't make any difference, Uncle Alex. And I do know you need Jesus. He wants to give you a big turnaround. He'll give you such great peace that you'll be able to face anything. And that's because He loves you."

He bowed his head and stared at the floor. "It's too good to be true," he said softly.

I reached over and patted his arm. "Maybe someday, Uncle Alex. Maybe someday you'll receive Jesus and experience His great love for you."

As I headed for the door and passed Aunt Amilda, I noticed she had big tears in her eyes. She hugged me tightly. "Oh, Marji, I do believe God sent you to us. We need something to change our lives. There must be more to life than this."

"That's why Jesus came, Aunt Amilda. To make life worth living."

"Well, maybe someday it'll happen to us. But I don't think we're ready yet. But you keep praying for us, will you?"

"Of course I will. You're my very dear aunt and uncle." I squeezed her.

"And you pray for me, will you? Pray that I'll find that counseling-center building."

Aunt Amilda nodded yes. Uncle Alex was still staring at the floor, oblivious of the blaring TV. I knew he was thinking. Thank God for that much progress!

I don't know how many blocks I walked. All the little storefronts were either occupied or burned out. But somewhere in the Lower East Side there had to be a place for me.

I'd walked a long time. Fearing that Uncle Alex would be worried about me after that run-in with Benny Barnes, I decided I'd better head back toward the apartment. But when I was about two blocks away from home, I stopped. I couldn't believe my eyes. Right before me was exactly what I was looking for, and it had a FOR-RENT sign in the window! I peered inside and could see it was a completely vacant room. I just couldn't believe it.

The sign didn't tell who to contact, so I started next door to inquire. Then I got the shock of my life. Next door was a pornography shop! A big sign outside read: LIVE SEX. That was strange. I didn't know there was dead sex. Disgusting!

I knew I shouldn't be seen in a place like that. If I was, the stories would start, and I would never be able to reach these people.

As I stood there, wondering what to do, a man walked out of the porno shop. "Hey, mister," I said, "do you know who is renting this place next door?"

"Nope," he replied, and kept on walking.

Just then another man started toward the porno shop. I tapped him on the shoulder as he passed me. He turned around, surprised. Then he flashed a big smile and grabbed me.

"No! No! No! I'm not that kind of girl! Let go of me!"

He laughed and relaxed his grip. "Sorry. I thought you were part of the act here. I thought this place had really picked up, with a good-looking chick like you!"

"No, all I wanted to know is who is renting the place next door. There's nothing on the sign."

"Well, come in with me. We'll ask Luigi."

He grabbed my arm and started to pull me inside. I jerked back. "No! No! I'd better just wait out here."

In a few minutes he came back with a fat, middle-aged man. "Uh, miss, this is Luigi Columbo. Luigi, this is the girl who was asking about the place next door. You know anything about it?"

Mr. Columbo's eyes narrowed. He sneered as he said, "Say, girl, what do you want with the place next door? You in the porno business?"

I laughed. "No, I'm not in the porno business."

"Hey! Hey! This ain't funny business around here. The last guy who rented that place tried to muscle in on my business. Can you imagine someone with the nerve to open a porno shop next to me? Well, let me tell you something, girl. That guy ain't around no more. Nobody messes with Luigi Columbo and gets away with it."

"But, Mr. Columbo, I'm here to do good for people, not to hurt people."

"Well, I don't know what you're up to, lady, but as long as you don't open up a porno shop or a house of prostitution, it's okay with me. But if you ever mess with my business in any way, it'll be all over for you, lady. I'm a hard-working man with a wife and kids to support. I got to make my money, and you got to make yours. But let's not run any competition. You hear?"

"Mr. Columbo, you've got me all wrong. I'll never run any competition with you. As far as I'm concerned, the porno business and prostitution are disgusting."

I had said the wrong thing. This time it was Luigi Columbo who grabbed me by the blouse and pulled me up close. "Now wait just one little minute, lady! Don't you start criticizing my legitimate business. Don't you know that people want a little fun? My business is just to give them that fun they want!"

He tightened his grip on my blouse, and I could feel the strain around my neck. I knew here was another person I'd better not cross!

Suddenly he relaxed his grip. "Okay, lady, now that we understand each other, what you want to put in that storefront?"

"A counseling center."

"A counseling center?" he screamed. "You one of them nutty do-gooders? I ain't never heard of such a thing!"

"Well, as I told you, I just want to help people."

He grabbed me by the blouse again. I had the urge to scream for the cops or to slap him across the face, but I knew that wouldn't get me anywhere.

"Listen, lady," he yelled at me. "Are you a front for the cops? Are you an undercover agent tryin' to get evidence on me? I ain't never heard of a counseling center. What kind of baloney is this?"

"Please, Mr. Columbo, you're choking me. Just relax, and I'll tell you where I'm coming from."

"Okay, but you better make it good, lady, or you won't be no more!" Then he let go.

"Now here's what I have in mind. A counseling center is a place where people can find Jesus as their Saviour and be set free from their sins. Jesus wants to give people peace like nothing in all this world can provide."

He laughed. "You're not just a do-gooder; you're one of those religious do-gooders! I seen your kind before. You won't last!"

He turned toward his customer. "That's just great! A religious nut next door! Oh, well, we'll run her out before she can ever open her Bible!"

"Tell me, Mr. Columbo. Do you own that storefront?"

"Why should I tell you that? You ask your God. Have Him tell you who owns it, huh?" He really thought that was clever and laughed uproariously.

I walked away. There was no sense in messing with him. He looked half-crazy, anyway.

Uncle Alex seemed relieved when I returned to the apartment. "I guess you had a safe journey," he said. "No muggings? No Benny Barnes?"

"Well, I managed to make it. But it was a little rough out there."

"Yeah, Marji, it gets real rough out there—every single day."

"Yes, but I found the storefront I want, and it's only two blocks away. It looks really nice."

Uncle Alex just took another sip from his beer. He didn't seem too interested, but I was going to tell him anyway.

"The place I found is right next to a porno shop, though."

"Very interesting. Next to a porno shop, hey? That's real competition, if you ask me."

"Well, I met the guy who owns the porno shop."

"Don't tell me, Marji. You went into one of those places? Goodness me, you're really going to get tainted with sin if you go in some place like that." He could be so sarcastic!

"No, nothing like that, Uncle Alex. In fact, we talked out on the street. The guy's name is Luigi Columbo."

Alex came flying out of his chair again. He slapped his beer can on the table and yelled, "Luigi Columbo? For crying out loud, Marji, you must specialize in getting yourself into deep trouble. Do you know who Luigi Columbo is?"

"No, I've never heard of him. Is he famous?"

"Is he famous? He's more than famous. There are two guys who are known as the meanest guys on the Lower East Side. One of them is Benny Barnes. You guess who the other is."

"I don't know. Probably the devil."

"Listen, Marji, this other guy is worse than the devil. His name is—and you get this straight—his name is Luigi Columbo!"

Well, I must say the Lord was really leading me to the people who needed Him most! In just a few hours

I'd met the two worst ones on the Lower East
Side!

"Furthermore, Marji, nobody messes with Luigi,
either! Do you know why that place next to his is for
rent? That's because nobody wants to go there, next to
Luigi. One stupid jerk tried it. He opened a porno
shop, and he didn't last a week. You know where they
found him? In the East River, with five bullet holes in
his skull! Everybody knows Luigi did it. But nobody
down here, and I mean *nobody,* is going to open his
mouth against Luigi Columbo. That would be the end
of him!"

My mouth flew open. I guess I really was flirting
with danger. And yet, what better place to open an
evangelistic center than next to a pornography shop?
Not Luigi Columbo, Benny Barnes, or any of the rest
of them were bigger than my God!

A spirit of what some people call righteous indigna-
tion swept over me. "That's it!" I declared. "That's it!
I'm going right back to that storefront and claim it for
God. Threats or no threats, I believe God wants me to
have that place."

Uncle Alex and Aunt Amilda looked as if they
thought I had lost my mind. No matter, I was mad at
the ways of evil; and I was going to claim a beachhead
for Christ.

In front of the empty storefront, I dropped on my
knees and started to pray out loud. I told God how
much He and I needed this place. All those girls who
were burdened with sin needed a place of peace and
rest. Those who walked these streets without any hope
could find hope in Jesus at this place. Their burdens

would be lifted, and people would be set free. I claimed it in the name of Jesus.

I was weeping as I slowly got to my feet. But I felt better. Then, through my tears, I could see him staring at me: Luigi Columbo!

"Listen, girl, I heard every word you said to that God of yours. Me, I don't believe in something I can't see. I don't believe in no God. I don't know who He is. But I know who Luigi Columbo is. No way are you going to operate any business or stupid counseling center in that store. Nobody, including you or your God, is going to mess up what I got goin' here."

I guess my prayer meeting must have made me act more boldly than I felt. I squared myself in front of him, looked him straight in the eye, and said, "Mr. Columbo, your days are numbered. God is on my side. He's going to help me open this counseling center. And if you fight it, God will make your business close. So be careful!"

Luigi stepped back and doubled over with laughter. "That's the funniest joke I've heard in twenty years! A little girl like you and your God are going to put *me* out of business? Tell me another!"

"Mr. Columbo, I'm very serious. I've just claimed this storefront for God, and I think He's going to give it to me. You'd better watch out!"

"Nobody threatens Luigi Columbo," he said menacingly, as he started back into his store. "Little girl, ever hear of the East River?"

I turned on my heels, did a complete about-face, and, with my head high, walked away.

Somehow God would help me find who owned that storefront. Somehow His message of love and help would be proclaimed in the Lower East Side. I knew it would!

I couldn't resist looking back to see what Luigi was doing. He had been watching me, and when he saw me turn around, he put his finger to his head, mimicking a gun. "East River, here you go, baby!" he yelled.

Any other time I would have shuddered with fear. But I just gritted my teeth and walked bravely away. After all, God was on my side, and He and I were going to see this through. But what would it cost me? And how was I going to find the owner of that storefront? That was my immediate problem. What if Luigi Columbo owned it? There would be no way he'd rent it to me!

8

With the threats I had already received, I had to accept the fact that it might cost me my life to open that counseling center. But at the moment I was feeling so brave that that really didn't matter. All I wanted was to see that counseling center opened as a testimony to God's power and grace in the Lower East Side—somehow, some way.

I headed back to the apartment. Maybe Uncle Alex would know who owned the storefront. I'd forgotten to ask him that.

I was almost to the end of the block when I heard footsteps running behind me. Oh, no! Not again! That would be Luigi Columbo coming after me—probably with his gun. All my brave thoughts about being a martyr suddenly vanished, and I took off, running as fast as I could.

The faster I ran, the faster the footsteps behind me moved. Was it a mugger? Did I dare look back? If it was Luigi and he was going to shoot me, I'd rather he'd shoot me in the back; and I would not have to see the blazing gun.

At the corner I bounded up the steps to my uncle's apartment. Oh, no! The door was locked! I listened intently for the footsteps—nothing. But I could hear someone panting heavily at the bottom of the stairs.

I slowly turned to face the sound, thinking this was probably it. But there stood a man I'd never seen before. I judged him to be about forty. He was beckoning me to come down the steps.

"No way!" I yelled.

He motioned again.

"Are you kidding?" I shouted.

Just then he pulled out a pencil and paper and wrote in big letters: COME HERE.

Then I figured out why my yelling wasn't doing any good: He was deaf.

I was so winded that I just took my time going down the steps. He smiled as I came toward him.

"I'm sorry," I said. "I didn't realize you were deaf."

Stupid me! Then I realized he couldn't hear that, either! I patted him on the shoulder and very slowly mouthed it, "I'm sorry."

He nodded and smiled.

I felt so ashamed. I wondered what he wanted.

"What do you want?" I asked, forgetting again that he couldn't hear me.

I reached for his paper and pencil and wrote my question.

He wrote out: I OWN STORE. YOU WANT TO RENT?

Talk about miracles! And it happened so quickly, too! How could he possibly know about me? He couldn't have heard Luigi and me yelling, because he was deaf!

So I wrote: HOW DO YOU KNOW?

He wrote: MY WIFE HEARD YOU. IT WAS VERY FUNNY.

So that was it!

It was futile trying to write everything out, so I

asked if I could talk to his wife.

He led me back to the building where the storefront was, and we went upstairs to their apartment. He began to use sign language to explain who I was to his wife. Then she came over to me.

"My name is Vivian Carlson. What is your name?"

"I'm Marji Parker. I'm very happy to meet you."

"This is my husband, Andrew, Marji. He wants you to know he's sorry if he frightened you. Now I understand you want to rent our vacant store downstairs."

"Yes, I would. How much are you asking for it?"

"Before I give you a price, I have to know what you want to use it for. We have had some bad things happen around here. One man rented it; he told us he wanted to open a grocery store. Instead, he opened a pornography shop. As you know, Luigi Columbo already has one next door, and it's a terrible thing on this block. The kind of people they draw there is indescribable. Well, we certainly don't want another one. And if Mr. Columbo has his way, we'll never have another one. The fellow who rented our store was murdered."

"Yes, I heard about that. My uncle Alex told me a few things about Mr. Columbo."

"Alex? You don't mean Alex Parker, do you?"

"Yes, he's my uncle."

"Oh, my goodness! A beautiful young lady like you, and he's your uncle?"

I smiled. "Well, I guess Uncle Alex wouldn't win any beauty contests, but every once in a while he does show some concern and love."

"I must tell you something about your uncle. Last winter Andrew and I found him out in the street, lying in the snow. We brought him up here and gave him some hot coffee to try to sober him up. It didn't do much good, so we had to put him in our bed. He was filthy and dirty, but we just couldn't let that man die in the street. Well, he slept off his drunkenness, and we had a chance to talk to him. He was thankful for what we had done, but he wouldn't accept any further help. He's a very proud man. I guess only God will be able to change him.''

"You said it, Mrs. Carlson. Only God can change his life.''

"Don't tell me, Marji; you're a Christian, aren't you?''

"Yes, I am. Are you, too?''

Mrs. Carlson threw her arms around me. "Praise the Lord! Isn't this wonderful? You're a Christian! This is absolutely amazing!''

She began to sign to her husband. His face lit up.

"Well, Marji, what are you going to use that storefront for? A church?''

"Well, not exactly, but close. I want to open a counseling center, so I can bring people in and talk to them about Jesus.''

"Praise the Lord! I think that's a wonderful idea!''

"Mrs. Carlson, I can't believe that on my first day here I've already met a couple of Christian friends. I knew there must be Christians around, but you're the first ones I've met.''

"There aren't too many down here. But if the three of us really seek God, I believe He will add to our group. This area really needs God's help!''

"That's what I'm here for. I believe God brought me to this place.''

"Just a minute, Marji. Let me talk to Andrew."

They made some signs back and forth, both of them smiling and very happy.

"Marji," she said, "since you're going to use this for a counseling center, Andrew and I will give you the best deal we can on it. We're living on Social Security, and we don't have too much, but God has been supplying our needs. We've been renting that storefront for four hundred dollars a month, but we've decided that, for you, we'll cut that in half. We'll consider that two hundred dollars is for the Lord, and we'll charge you the other two hundred dollars. Does that seem right?"

"Oh, that's beautiful, just beautiful! My father said he would help me with the rent."

"Is your father a minister?"

"No, he's not a minister. I wish he was. He's a . . . a . . . a . . . a . . ."

I didn't want to tell them my dad was a millionaire. I didn't really know what to say. So I finally said, "Let's just say he's a good man."

"Well, I think that's wonderful. I'll bet he's real proud of you."

"Well, he really wasn't anxious for me to come down here. But my folks are behind me, and I'm trying to help my uncle Alex. I really believe God is going to save him."

"Andrew and I have been praying for him, Marji. Maybe God sent you here to answer those prayers."

We talked about what I was planning to do. Then they took me downstairs and showed me through the building. I visualized myself sitting at a desk, with people coming in for help. It seemed too good to be true.

I told the Carlsons I would have to check with my father, but that this place seemed to be just right for what I needed. We said good-bye. They headed back upstairs, and I started the two blocks to Uncle Alex's apartment.

This time I didn't hear any footsteps behind me. Instead, I felt an arm tighten around my throat. And I heard a voice I would recognize anywhere: "Listen, kid, you didn't take me seriously, did you? How did you find the Carlsons?"

I squirmed, but the grip tightened. Luigi had a lot of power in his grip.

"I'm not messing with you anymore. I warned you. Now I'm going to teach you a lesson and teach you good!"

I tried to scream, but his grip was shutting off my wind.

He pushed me down the street, by a tenement house, and into a vacant lot. It was dirty and smelly. There was garbage all around.

He forced me against the side of the building and then whirled me around, his hands still tight against my throat. Then he screamed, "I told you to get out of here. I saw you with the Carlsons. Well, let me tell you, no way are you going to live to rent that storefront! You hear me?"

I guess he felt obligated to give me a chance to say something, because he relaxed his grip on my throat.

"Now, Mr. Columbo," I said, "let's be reasonable. I'm not going to open a porno shop. I'm not going to open a house of prostitution. I'm just trying to help people. Can't you believe that?"

"You religious nuts are all alike. Next thing I know, you'll be out there picketing my shop. Nobody's going to threaten me. You understand that?"

"Listen, Mr. Columbo, let's work a deal. I'll go ahead and open my counseling center, and let's see what happens. I believe that when people come to know Jesus as their Saviour, their quality of life will improve. Why, if everybody here on the Lower East Side got to know Jesus, there'd be no more muggings, no rapes, no killings, or other types of problems like that. It would be so peaceful, so different. You want that, don't you?"

He grabbed my throat again. "Listen, kid, you got a lot to learn. I ain't out to make peace in the world. I'm out to make a buck. I could care less what happens to the Lower East Side and all the crud that lives here. But I do care what happens to my business. I got a good thing goin', and no little religious do-gooder with stars in her eyes is going to spoil it. You hear?"

I nodded. "I just wish you wouldn't push so hard against my neck, Mr. Columbo. It really hurts!"

He relaxed his grip, and I said, "Okay, is it a deal?"

"No!" he screamed. "Absolutely no deal. If you try to open up that place, you're going to suffer terrible consequences!"

His threats made me all the more determined to open that center. No porno-shop owner was going to stop me from doing what I felt God wanted me to do. So with more boldness than wisdom I declared, "Mr. Columbo, your threats don't worry me. I'm going to open up that counseling center for Jesus, whether you like it or not!"

I guess no one had ever stood up to him before,

because he went absolutely berserk! He raised his fist
to hit me. I jumped, and he hit the wall instead. That
infuriated him even more! Then I saw his foot coming,
and I jumped again. Again he missed. But he didn't
miss the building!

I saw my chance to run for it, but as I turned, I
slipped on some garbage and fell. He lunged and
landed right on top of me. He raised his fist, and I tried
to duck. Then I felt his hands tighten around my
throat. Tighter. Tighter . . . .

No screams would come. Was this going to be the
end of my dream? It seemed as if it was getting darker
and darker. I tried to kick and to squirm, but Luigi had
me pinned down.

I knew this was it. I had told the Lord I was ready to
die for Him. He must have been listening! But I really
hadn't expected it to happen on my first day!

My body started to go limp. I couldn't resist . . . .

Just then I heard a loud smack, and I felt the weight
of Luigi's body go hurdling off me. I could hear him
screaming.

Very, very slowly I sat up. I could see him clutching
his head, obviously in severe pain. My vision cleared,
and I saw another figure nearby. Slowly it all came into
focus. I saw a Catholic nun. What was that in her
hand? It looked like a two-by-four.

She walked over to me. "Honey, are you all right?"
I couldn't believe it. How could I still be alive?

"I beg your pardon?" I said.

"I asked if you were okay."

I turned and looked down at Luigi, as she helped me
to my feet. He was still holding his head and howling

with pain. I turned back to the nun and said, "Yeah, I guess so. What happened?"

"I was walking along and just happened to look down here," she said. "I saw you and Mr. Columbo in this terrible fight, and I thought I'd better come over and even the score. I know him. He may mess with a lot of people, but he's not going to mess with me!"

The nun raised her two-by-four again and walked over toward Luigi. He yelled, "Sister, Sister, please don't hit me again! This little nut was trying to ruin my business!"

She looked at me. "I don't know what you're up to, young lady, but if you're trying to ruin his porno business, you can't be all bad."

"Aw, come on, Sister," Luigi interjected. "I got a legitimate business. I give people a little fun. That can't be wrong."

"Let me tell you about Mr. Columbo," she said to me. "Ever since he opened that shop, I've been trying my best to get it closed. But it seems as if the more I work on it, the more people come to it. I just don't know what to do."

"Well, Sister," I said, "I just can't believe you took that two-by-four and clobbered him on the head."

She laughed. "I figured that with God on my side and a two-by-four in my hand, I could·settle that argument pretty quickly. I'm not afraid of Luigi Columbo!"

I had to admire the spunk of this Catholic sister. I had read that nuns had gone to difficult places all over the world and had given their lives to help people. This one evidently was trying to help people in the Lower

East Side. I was anxious to get to know more about her.

By this time Luigi was edging away from us. As he got to the safety of the street, he yelled, "Okay, you two religious nuts. You may have won this time, but I'm going to get both of you!"

The nun picked up the two-by-four and started toward him. Luigi didn't lose any time getting away!

"Thanks, Sister. I believe you must be one of God's guardian angels. You saved my life! By the way, I'm Marji Parker."

"Marji, I'm Sister Mary Pat."

She started brushing the dirt off my clothes. I ran a comb through my hair to try to make myself look presentable. While she was helping me, she asked what I had done to anger Luigi so much.

"Well," I told her, "I'm planning to start a counseling center next door to his shop. I want to be able to talk to the girls around here and show them how Jesus can help them."

"Marji, you and I need to talk. Let's go get a cup of coffee."

"Sounds like a great idea!"

A couple of blocks away we found a small coffee shop. When we got comfortably settled, I began to tell her about myself and the center I hoped to open.

As we talked, I learned that she had been down on the Lower East Side for five years. She had been raised in Illinois, but even as a teenager she had been burdened to help poor people. She certainly had found them here!

"Then about two years ago," she told me, "I had a deep hunger in my heart for more of the Lord. I was so frustrated that I wasn't able to do more to help people.

Well, someone invited me to a Bible study uptown, on Sixty-Eighth Street. A friend of mine told me that some very interesting things were happening there.''

I nodded. Small Bible studies were spreading rapidly around the country, and people were being helped by them.

"Now, Marji, I don't know if you will really understand this, but something remarkable happened to me. After the Bible study, the man conducting it asked if any of us wanted to receive the baptism in the Holy Spirit. I didn't recognize that term, so he explained again that God wanted Christians to have more power to help them be better witnesses. Well, I needed all the help I could get.''

"Oh, Sister Mary Pat, I know all about the baptism in the Holy Spirit. What happened to you?''

A big smile lit up her face. "That night the Lord gloriously filled me with the Holy Spirit! And, Marji, my life has been so different ever since. And I've been able to see more accomplished for the Lord than ever before!''

"Well, Sister, I, too, am Spirit-filled!''

"Praise the Lord!'' she said. "It's always wonderful to meet another Spirit-filled believer!

"Well then, Marji, are you developing the fruit of the Spirit in your life?''

"I guess so,'' I said as I pondered her unexpected question. "No, I guess I'm really lacking. Why do you ask?''

"Well, it's about that Luigi Columbo. You see, I know all about him. I understand he's killed people who get in his way. But, Marji, I'm not a bit afraid of him.

"Now the first time I heard of him, I was scared to death. I knew that I was fighting not only Mr. Columbo and his porno shop, but I was also fighting the devil. The devil doesn't want that porno shop closed."

She was right. I guess I had been thinking only of Luigi Columbo and not of the evil powers that were using him.

"Well, Marji, part of the fruit of the Spirit is peace. I was in so much fear concerning Mr. Columbo that I almost left the Lower East Side. But I asked God for a miracle. He took out that fear of Mr. Columbo and put His peace inside me. He can do that for you, too."

She was so right. It was exactly what I needed to hear. I couldn't allow Luigi Columbo or Benny Barnes or anyone else to stop me. Somehow we had to win these people to Jesus Christ. I could trust God to take care of me. Look at what He had already done for me today!

We talked for a long time. She told me she was associated with the Saint Thomas Catholic Church. When we finally got up to leave, she told me, "Now, Marji, don't you dare worry about Luigi Columbo. God is on your side."

"I'll try not to. And I'm certainly going to ask God to give me that peace you were talking about."

"It'll come. Just trust the Lord, and it'll come."

"But, Sister Mary Pat, supposing, just supposing, Luigi Columbo did kill you. What then?"

Without flinching she said, "Well, wouldn't that be just wonderful? Of course I know what then. I would go to heaven!"

She stood there with a triumphant look on her face. "And, Marji, if he killed you, what then?"

''Let's hope that if he kills us, he'll kill us both at the same time. Then we can enjoy heaven together!''

We both laughed and then went our separate ways. As I walked toward the apartment, in the gathering darkness, I thought of Luigi Columbo. Maybe he was waiting around the corner. And I was still scared!

9

The next few weeks were filled with work. It had seemed so easy when I had given the rental check to the Carlsons. I thought I would simply have to open the door, and I would be in business. I quickly learned differently! There was so much cleaning up to do. And I had to find furniture.

The Carlsons' church gave me some old furniture. It wasn't much, but the old chairs provided a place for people to sit down—broken springs and all. And the old desk gave me a place to keep my papers.

Finally the counseling center was ready. Of course, things were pretty slow at first.

Every so often Uncle Alex would drop by, and we would have some tremendous conversations. I gather he had been quite a thinker. Now I sensed the Lord was really beginning to work in his heart. Every day I prayed that he would receive Christ as his Saviour. But somehow I didn't feel I should press the issue yet.

Then one day he caught me by surprise. "Marji," he said, "I think it's about time for you to end your little dream and go back home."

"What?" I exclaimed. "What are you talking about? I've only had the center open for four weeks. Naturally I haven't seen any results yet. I just can't close up and leave!"

He just stood there, sort of kicking at a hole in the carpet.

"What's the matter, Uncle Alex? Don't you and Aunt Amilda want me living with you anymore?"

"Oh, no," he quickly responded. "Nothing like that at all."

"Then what is it?"

"Marji, I don't know if I should tell you this or not, but on the street the word is that some people are going to try to get you."

"Oh, Uncle Alex, don't start that again. I haven't seen Benny Barnes from that first day, and I've seen Luigi Columbo only twice. He's steered clear of me since that nun clobbered him!"

Alex walked over to my desk, bent across it, and looked me straight in the eye. "Marji, it isn't over between you and Benny and Luigi. One of them is setting up something to knock you off. I tried to find out which one, but my friend wouldn't tell me. He just said to tell you to keep your eyes open because it's going to happen one of these days."

"Please, Uncle Alex, don't worry. Nothing is going to happen to me. Look how God has taken care of me so far!"

"Come on, Marji! Everybody's luck runs out one day! I want you to get out of here before you get it. If it's Benny, he'll break your arms and legs and stab you to death. If it's Luigi, he'll blow your brains out and throw you in the East River. Those guys are killers. You can't mess with them and get by with it!"

He was really upsetting me. "Uncle Alex, how can you ask me to leave? Don't you know there are people down here who need to know about the Lord? I haven't even really started yet, and now you're telling me to leave! Well, if I'm going to get killed, I'd rather it would be down here, where I'm doing what I feel the Lord wants me to do!" I said it with more bravery than I really felt!

"Marji, Marji! Please, please, listen to me!" he begged. "You know that people die around here all the time. And you're marked. I mean, even tonight it could happen. Don't you understand? *They're going to kill you!*"

"Uncle Alex, you're the one who doesn't understand. I'm not afraid to die."

He was getting more frustrated by the conversation. "If you weren't such a fine Christian lady, I'd turn this air blue! I guess I can even begin to understand that you're not afraid to die. I've heard other Christians say that. But in such a horrible way?"

I sat there in silence. I just wished that somehow he could grasp how I felt about these people.

"Marji, if you're so hung up on helping these people, why don't you go around to churches and college campuses and enlist young people to come down here? That way you'd be multiplying your life instead of trying to do everything yourself. Why don't you think about that?"

Not a bad idea. But how many young people would be willing to come? And how would they be supported? Besides, if I were going to do something like that, I had better have some experience at it myself before I asked someone else to do it! Maybe someday I would travel to Bible colleges and challenge young people to spend part of their lives down here. But not until I had seen some results from my own work, first.

"Listen, Uncle Alex, I don't see any point in arguing about this. I appreciate your concern, and that really makes me love you even more. But I have to stay."

"Marji, have you ever thought about all that money your dad is going to leave you one of these days? If you were dead, you wouldn't get a dime of it. If you were alive, you could use it down here in the ghetto. And you could live happily ever after, too!"

I laughed. "Uncle Alex, you know as well as I do that money isn't the solution to the world's problems. If it were, all the rich people would be happy and all the poor people would be sad. It just doesn't work that way, and you know it."

As he started out the front door, he turned and said, "Well, I'm going to keep a better eye out for you. When you close the counseling office at five, I'll be down to get you and walk you home. I don't want anything to happen to my favorite niece!"

"Oh, Uncle Alex, you're so sweet. You may not be the handsomest man in the world, but I really love you for trying to take care of me."

He grinned sheepishly.

I really was becoming fond of him. If somehow he'd just get saved. Maybe someday . . . .

After that conversation, every evening at five Uncle Alex would be waiting for me. We'd walk home together, and it gave me that many more opportunities to get to know him better and to talk to him about Jesus. He opened up a little concerning all the hurts related to my father, and once again I had a chance to emphasize Dad's desire to treat him right. Slowly the bitterness seemed to leave. Now if he would just open his heart and replace that bitterness with Christ's love . . . .

I didn't expect people simply to walk into the counseling center, so I began to spend some evenings on the streets, trying to talk to some of the girls. Uncle Alex always insisted on going out with me, but he had enough sense to stay about thirty feet away.

He was so patient. Sometimes I would spend several hours out there, and he would be out there, leaning up against a building, watching out for me. Bless his heart! I always felt more secure when he was around.

He knew that most of the action took place at night, especially with all the prostitutes out on the street.

Every so often I'd see Patsy. Without making a big scene out of it—because of Benny—I tried to talk to her. She always seemed willing to listen, but I never could get much of a response. Usually she would say something like, "Some other time."

That's probably why I was so surprised one day when I was at my desk at the counseling center, and Patsy walked in.

"Patsy, I'm so glad to see you again. What brings you down here?"

She started to cry. I jumped out of my chair and went over and put my arms around her to try to quiet her. "Patsy, what's the matter?"

By this time she was sobbing so hard that she couldn't answer me. I guided her over to the sofa and sat down beside her, quietly waiting for her to open up.

When she had finally calmed down to an occasional sob, I asked again, "Patsy, what's the matter?"

Her eyes were red. She had been crying before she came here. Her face was pale as death. Between the sobs, she forced out the words, "Oh, Marji! I think I have come to the end. I just can't take this life anymore. I'm going to end it all!"

"No, Patsy! That's no solution."

"It's the only way out for me," she wailed. "Benny is out there looking for me right now. Last night I walked out on that pimp, and I'm never going back. He didn't know I left him when I walked out on him at three this morning. But he knows now. I saw a couple of his girls, and they said he was looking for me. I know I'm going to be number six. He'll kill me, Marji! Better I kill myself first!"

What was I going to do? How could I help this distraught wisp of a girl who had squandered her life in prostitution?

"Please, Marji, if you only knew what I've been through. Please, isn't there something you can do to help me?"

She threw her arms around me as if she was grasping at her final hope.

At the moment all I could do was hold her close. She seemed so frail, so helpless, so vulnerable.

I was also keeping one eye on the door. I knew that any minute now Benny could come bursting in, and that would be the end of Patsy and maybe of me. I had to think of something, quick!

"Please, please, can't you help me?" Patsy begged again.

I breathed another of those quick prayers. "Patsy," I said, "I'm sure God has a way out of this, but I don't know what it is yet."

Then I thought of an answer. Why not send Patsy up to the Walter Hoving Home in Garrison, New York—just as the people did for Cindy, in John Benton's book? I was sure they would take her in. Of course, that was the answer! Why hadn't I thought of it sooner?

But how was I going to do it? We could take a train, but how was I going to smuggle her out of the Lower East Side and onto that train? I could even go with her to be sure everything was okay. But the big problem was that Benny was out there, right now, looking for her. We couldn't just walk to the subway in broad daylight.

Sometimes, in a crisis, people get crazy ideas. I did in this one. I thought that if I could find a big box to put her in, I could carry her out.

Now that I had a plan, I was ready to share it with Patsy.

"I think there is something I can do to help you," I told her. "There's a program for drug addicts and alcoholics at the Walter Hoving Home, upstate in Garrison. I've been in touch with the director before. I know they would let you stay there and take care of you. You'd be safe there. It's a one-year program, and I know you would like it."

"What kind of place is it?"

"You know how I've talked with you on the street about Jesus? Well, the Home is a place where girls study the Bible and apply its teachings to their lives. They call it a Christ-centered program. I believe it would be the best thing in the world for you. Not only will it save you from Benny Barnes, but Jesus will change your life completely. You'll discover there really is something worth living for!"

"I certainly need something, Marji. I can't go on like I've been doing. I feel so empty, so dirty. But do you think we can make it up there?"

"Let's pray about it." We did.

Then I told her about my idea of the big box. "I'll lock the door while I'm gone, but I want you to crawl underneath my desk and hide there. If anybody comes, don't move. It could be Benny!"

As soon as I said *Benny,* Patsy headed for the desk and crawled underneath.

I must have walked four blocks before I finally spied a box I thought would do the trick. It was sitting on the showroom floor of a furniture store.

Inside, I asked the clerk, "Could I have that box sitting over there?"

"Yeah, I guess so. What are you going to do with it? You moving?"

"Well, not exactly," I answered. "Yeah, I guess you might call it that. Moving, yeah, that's what it is."

"Sure, you can have it. I hope you move to a better place!"

It seemed as if everybody wanted out of the Lower East Side.

The salesman helped me get the box out onto the street. Then I started off toward the counseling center, going as quickly as I dared. I really couldn't see where I was going, so when I rounded a corner, I slammed into a man. He was a big, burly fellow, and I bounced off him and went sailing across the sidewalk. The man didn't even stop to see if I was hurt. But as I was picking myself up, that's when I saw a familiar figure: Benny Barnes!

I gasped. He walked over and stood there threateningly. I wasn't fully on my feet yet, and now I was too scared to get up.

It was like slow motion. He reached into his coat pocket. Then he bent over and opened his hand, revealing a large switchblade. He pushed the little trigger, and the blade snapped toward me. It looked as if that blade were eighteen inches long!

He bent over a little farther, and I felt the point of the blade touch my throat.

I wanted to scream for the police. I guess he anticipated that, because he pushed the point of the blade up under my chin. I felt it prick the skin.

"Listen, preacher lady, I'm lookin' for Patsy. You seen her?"

What was I going to do? Should I lie and say no? Should I tell the truth? If I lied, I'd be in trouble with the Lord. If I told the truth, Patsy would probably be killed, and I'd be responsible for someone's death.

I was afraid to open my mouth for fear the tip of his switchblade would jab deeper into my throat. So I slowly raised my hand to his and tried to push the blade away gently.

I felt his grip tighten. He wasn't about to move.

I let my hands settle at my side.

"Listen, preacher lady, I'm going to ask you once again: Have you seen Patsy?"

Oh, God, what am I going to do? I don't want to lie, and I couldn't tell Patsy's hiding place.

Then an idea struck me. It was a chance, but it was worth a try.

I rolled my eyes, slowly stuck out my tongue, and went completely limp, pretending I had fainted. I held my breath and let my head gently roll to the side. I pushed my tongue out a little more.

"Hey, preacher lady, nobody's going to pass out on me!"

I felt him slap my face, but I just let my body roll as limply as possible.

Then I felt him give me a vicious kick. Trying to stay limp, I rolled with that, too. By this time I had rolled off the curb and into the gutter. My face was in the dirt, and I was almost nauseated by the stench. But I had to play through my act. Otherwise it would have been the end of me and of Patsy.

"Listen, you little twerp, I ought to throw you in the river. That would wake you up. Either you're a good faker or you really have fainted. But if you're listening to me and you know where Patsy is, I'm going to tell you something. I'll teach that Patsy a lesson she'll never forget. I mean *never*. If you see her, tell her that!"

I didn't dare open my eyes, but I heard footsteps moving away from me. I hoped it was Benny. But what if he had just walked a short distance away to watch me?

I don't know how long I was there in the gutter, but the next thing I remember was someone's hand on my shoulder, pushing me. "Hey, wake up! Marji! Wake up!"

I recognized that voice. There was Sister Mary Pat bent over me.

I reached up and threw my arms around her. "Oh, Sister Mary Pat, God has sent you again to me—and at just the right time!"

"Well, what happened this time? Did a truck hit you?"

"No, it was Benny Barnes. He was out to get me, and I just had to pull a little fake. I faked fainting."

"Well, if nothing else, you may end up being a good actress. I couldn't believe my eyes, seeing you lying there in the gutter. I couldn't imagine what you were doing down there. Certainly not leading souls to Christ!"

I laughed. Then I slowly got up, straightened my clothes and my hair, and looked for my box. It was still sitting there. I had half expected it to be gone.

I wondered if I should tell Sister Mary Pat about Patsy. Would she tell anyone else? Probably not, but I decided that I'd better keep it a secret.

"I was just taking this box to my counseling center, Sister, and I ran into Benny Barnes. He's upset about one of his girls."

"You watch out for that Benny Barnes," she warned.

"Oh, I'll be careful. Sorry I can't talk any more now. I've got to hurry. See you later." And with that I grabbed my box and started running down the street—but this time I was a little more careful to watch where I was going!

Back at the counseling center, I let myself in and locked the door behind me. "Patsy, it's me," I whispered.

I told her about my encounter with Benny, and I thought she was going to pass out on me!

Next I sneaked her into the big box and shut the lid. So far, so good. Then I tried to pick up the box. Suddenly it hit me what a stupid idea this was. No way was I going to be able to pick up that box with Patsy inside!

I strained. I huffed and puffed. It was all I could do to push it a little way across the floor. Finally I gave one big shove, with all my might, and the box tumbled over and ripped. That was the end of that brilliant idea!

Patsy slithered out of the beat-up box and crawled back under the desk. "Please, Marji," she said, her voice choking with desperation. "Please, can't you think of something else?"

I needed time to think. I decided I might as well get rid of that box. If I went to throw it out, maybe I'd get another idea; I hoped it would be something that would work!

I dragged the tattered box out the front door to a garbage can. I turned, and as I did, I glanced across the street. There, leaning up against a building, keeping watch on my counseling center, was Benny Barnes.

He saw me! "Hey, preacher lady," he yelled, "I see you revived. Well, you won't stay healthy long!"

I darted back inside the counseling center, quickly locking the door behind me.

"Patsy, Benny is across the street!"

"Oh, no!" she wailed. "I'm dead! I'm dead!"

What was I to do now? There was no way I could sneak Patsy out the door.

I paced through the office, glancing out the window every now and then to see if Benny was still there. He was; and he was cleaning his fingernails with that long switchblade. It looked hideous.

I was praying as I was pacing, and another idea came to me. It was a little farfetched, too, I realized. But it sounded a lot better than the box idea.

"Patsy, you stay in your hiding place," I whispered. "I've got another idea for getting you out of here. I'll be back in a few minutes."

Patsy looked at me skeptically. I guess she didn't

think too much of my ideas. But she really had no choice.

I gingerly opened the door. Benny wasn't looking at me right now. I squeezed out, locked the door again, and took off running. I just knew he would start chasing me. But he didn't. I knew he saw me, though, because he yelled after me: "Hey, preacher lady, better be careful runnin' like that. It might make you pass out!"

I could still hear his sinister laughter as I took off toward Sister Mary Pat's church. There was no time to lose!

10

I ran the four blocks to Saint Thomas Catholic Church. Sister Mary Pat just *had* to be there. Right now she was my only hope for getting Patsy out of the city and up to the Walter Hoving Home.

I went to the front doors of the church—all locked. I wasn't too surprised at that. Muggers even knock off churches on the Lower East Side.

I tried a side door, and it opened into a hallway where the church offices were. But no one was around.

I knocked on some of the office doors—no answer. I tried them—all locked. I was beginning to panic. Somehow I had to find Sister Mary Pat. But how? And where?

I tried another door and found myself in the sanctuary. Ordinarily I would have stopped to look at the beauty of the place, but not now. My footsteps echoed as I walked up to the altar. It was as still as death otherwise.

I half ran back into the hallway and knocked desperately on some more doors—nothing.

What was I going to do now? I could yell, but in a church? It seemed so inappropriate! Never mind! I had to find Sister Mary Pat. So I yelled her name as loudly as I could.

Her name bounced off the bare walls and floor and echoed around and around. It sounded as if an army were calling her!

But it worked! I heard footsteps running toward me. I started in the direction of the sound, and when I turned a corner, there was Sister Mary Pat!

"Marji, what in the world are you doing here? Child, you look upset. What's wrong? What do you need?"

"One question at a time, please," I said, trying to be as nonchalant as possible. "I just needed to ask a special favor of you, and since there wasn't anybody around to tell me how to reach you, I used my own public-address system!"

"Well, it worked, Marji. What's the favor?"

"I need you to come with me to my counseling center right away."

"Is that all? Of course. But why don't we just step into one of these offices and talk? It's quiet here, and we wouldn't have anyone interfering or interrupting. Would that be okay?"

That wasn't what I had in mind! I had to get her to that counseling center.

"Oh, that's very kind of you, but it isn't just that I want to talk to you. I have something special that I want to show you at the center."

She looked puzzled. "Does it have something to do with that huge box?"

"Well, yes and no."

"My, you're a helpful one today, aren't you?"

"Well, let's just say it's not something Santa Claus would bring, and it's not a special blessing from the Pope. But if I tell you what it is, it won't be a surprise!"

"I can't argue with that logic," she said.

I knew she was trying to figure out what I was up to. But I had to get her down to the counseling center without telling her that Patsy was hiding there or that Benny was standing across the street.

"Now to make this a little more interesting," I said, "could you please get a pair of sunglasses and wear them to my office?"

"Come on, Marji. This is really getting mysterious!"

What else could I say? Maybe I should just tell her that she needed to come to the counseling center to save a soul. But I had more than Patsy's soul in mind!

Instead I said, "Sister Mary Pat, I know you really must love the people down here on the Lower East Side. But have you ever wondered what it would feel like to be one of them?"

"Yes, I have. I think at times I am able to show empathy, but sometimes I wonder what it is really like being born down here and having to live in these horrible surroundings."

"Well, that's part of my secret. I've found a way to give you an opportunity to really feel like one of them."

"Now, listen, Marji. I know you've got something up your sleeve . . . ."

"Okay, this is your chance of a lifetime," I interrupted. "If you come to the counseling center, I guarantee you're going to have one of the greatest experiences of your life. Trust me."

"Marji, I know I can trust you."

Suddenly she said, "Come on, kid! Let's go get 'em!"

We started toward the door. "Oh, just a minute! You forgot the sunglasses! Do you have a pair?"

"I do. Wait right here. They're up in my room."

"Hurry!"

Her nun's habit billowed behind her as she ran to her room. In a few minutes she was back.

"I hope I wasn't gone too long and spoiled my surprise!"

Was she ever going to be surprised!

As we stepped out the door, I asked her to put on the sunglasses.

"Put on the sunglasses? Oh, Marji! You're not serious, are you?"

"Yes, please put on the sunglasses."

"But, Marji, it's about ready to rain this morning, and you want me to wear sunglasses? Are you crazy?"

I smiled. "Probably I'm a little crazy. I know it looks ridiculous, but you've got to play the part."

As she stood there, studying me, not knowing whether I was joking or not, I reached over, took the sunglasses out of her hand, and slipped them on her face. It did look kind of stupid, but I didn't dare tell her that.

Sometimes people wear sunglasses to hide a shiner. They really cover up a black eye. I noticed people glancing at Sister Mary Pat as we walked along. Were they wondering how a nun got a black eye?

When we got down by the counseling center, Sister Mary Pat noticed Benny leaning up against the wall across the street. "Marji," she said as she tugged my elbow. "Look over there! That looks like . . . ." And she started to pull off her sunglasses to get a better look.

"No! Keep those glasses on!" I ordered in a whisper. "That's only Benny Barnes."

"What is he doing up against that wall? Knowing him, I'm sure he's up to no good."

Just then Benny saw us. "Hey, preacher lady, you takin' that nun in to convert her, too?" He really thought he was hilarious.

"Marji, you wait right here. I'm going over to give him a piece of my mind. I won't take a remark like that!"

I grabbed Sister Mary Pat's arm just in time. "Hold everything, Sister. If I recall, you were talking to me about the fruit of the Spirit, a little while ago. Let's exercise some of it and not get ourselves into trouble. Let's just leave Mr. Barnes up against the wall over there. Come on in the counseling center. I've got a surprise."

"Well, all right. But if I hear one more remark out of him, I'm going to get a two-by-four, and you know what I can do with that!"

I knew well. And so did Luigi Columbo. Yes, Sister Mary Pat probably could clobber Benny Barnes, too—but not now and not in that way.

I unlocked the center and then locked the door behind us. I pointed toward my desk. "Your surprise is under there." She bent over and then jerked up. "Well, whatever do we have here?"

"Patsy, come on out. I want you to meet a friend of mine."

Patsy crawled out from underneath the desk, careful to keep herself hidden from the front window.

"Patsy, this is Sister Mary Pat from Saint Thomas Church. Sister Mary Pat, this is Patsy. She needs help. And Sister, you can take your sunglasses off now!"

"I forgot I had them on. I guess my eyes got used to walking around in an eclipse!"

She and I laughed. But Patsy was too scared to

laugh. Sister Mary Pat could tell the girl was in trouble.

"Is this why you brought me down here, Marji?"

"Well, kind of. Patsy is one of Benny Barnes' girls, and she wants to get away. I'm trying to get her out of the city and up to the Walter Hoving Home, in Garrison."

"Oh, yes, I've heard about their work. But we do have a problem here, don't we? Especially with Benny standing across the street."

"Yes, we have a problem, but I believe there is a solution to it."

"This looks to me like the time for a prayer meeting," Sister Mary Pat said. "I'm sure God will direct us."

That was something I liked about Sister Mary Pat. She was always so full of faith.

"Sister, I've already prayed, and I believe God has given me the answer."

"Well, praise the Lord, girl! What is it?"

I stood there, looking lovingly at Sister Mary Pat. Could I really ask her to do it?

"Come on, Marji! What's the solution?"

I should have chosen my words more carefully. As it was, they came out, "Sister Mary Pat, would you mind taking off your clothes?"

She jumped back horrified. "Marji, how dare you suggest something nasty like that! Have you no respect?"

"I'm sorry. It didn't come out quite the way I intended."

She stood there, hands on her hips, waiting for my explanation.

"You see, Sister, this is what I think we should do. I

want you to exchange clothes with Patsy. You're both close to the same size. And you know those sunglasses you brought? When Patsy puts your clothes and those sunglasses on, she will look just like you. Then she and I will walk right out that front door. Benny will think that Patsy is you, and we can escape. Don't you think it will work?''

''Sounds super!'' Patsy responded.

But Sister Mary Pat wasn't so sure. ''Marji, you don't know what you're asking of me. If the mother superior found out I was a party to helping someone impersonate a Catholic sister, she would have my hide!''

''I can certainly understand that rule,'' I responded. ''I've heard about women in this city who impersonate nuns and go out on the streets, begging.''

''Yes, that has made our order absolutely furious. It is despicable!''

''Well, I can certainly understand your reluctance, Sister. But you know as well as I do what happens to these girls if they try to leave their pimps. Benny will kill Patsy. She'll be the sixth notch on his switchblade. And if Patsy got killed, you wouldn't want to have that on your conscience, would you? knowing that you had a chance to help her, but refused to, just because of your clothes?''

I had her there. I knew she knew that her nun's habit wasn't worth more than a human life. But just to be sure, I said, ''Sister, don't you remember what Jesus said about all this? If someone asks us for our cloak, we should give him our coat, too. I'm just asking you to do what Jesus said you should do.''

Slowly Sister Mary Pat began to disrobe. She didn't

say a word. I felt so sorry for her. I knew what I was asking her to do went against everything she had been taught. But she also knew the value of a life, in God's sight.

Patsy stripped off her jeans and blouse quickly. As she put on Sister Mary Pat's robes, I saw her face brighten for the first time that day. It reminded me of the way she had looked when she put on the coat I had given her.

"Hey, this really feels good!" Patsy said. "Maybe I ought to become a nun!"

I looked over at Sister, struggling to get into Patsy's tight-fitting blue jeans. "Sister Mary Pat, I think you'd make a good prostitute!"

"Marji, that is not funny at all!"

"Hey, I think it is," Patsy said. "You could make a lot of money on the street!"

Patsy and I laughed, but Sister Mary Pat stood there, staring icily at us.

I felt so embarrassed. I knew I'd offended her, and I really hadn't intended to. It was just that the whole situation somehow seemed so ridiculous.

"I'm sorry, Sister. I didn't mean what I said. Would you please forgive me?"

She broke into tears and nodded. I felt so ashamed of myself—and not just for what I had said. Maybe I was asking too much of this dear woman.

Sister Mary Pat began to rub her hands over the clothing she was now wearing. Through her tears she looked over at me. "You know, Marji, I feel so strange with Patsy's clothes on. It seems as though, when I slipped them on, I almost became Patsy. I feel so lost and without hope. So naked and unclean. My religious garments were a cloak, but now it seems as though I stand before the world without any security, with nothing to hide behind. Patsy, is that the way you sometimes feel?"

Patsy stood there demurely in Sister Mary Pat's habit. "It's strange that you say that, Sister. I feel so secure and strong wearing your clothes. It really does something for me just to have these on. Do you know what I mean?"

As I looked at both of them, I thought: *What a paradox! Patsy now is the secure nun, and Sister Mary Pat is the bewildered prostitute.* It was very strange indeed. But the big question now was: Will it work?

"Just before we go, why don't we join hands and have prayer once again?" I suggested. "Let's believe God is going to get us all through this safely."

We bowed our heads, and I led the prayer: "Lord Jesus, I want to thank You that You do speak to us. I believe I heard You speaking when You told me about this plan. And now, Lord, I pray that somehow You will cover each of us with Your blood so that no harm will come to Patsy as we leave this counseling center. Somehow, Lord, make it possible for us to get through.

"And, Lord, thank You for Sister Mary Pat. She's such a wonderful Christian, who is willing to give all, even in these circumstances. Bless her in a special way. I know that You really love her for her sacrifice and her spirit of giving. Now we commit Patsy and Sister Mary Pat to You. Amen."

As I opened my eyes, I looked first at Patsy and noticed tears rolling down her cheeks. "Oh, I have such a great desire to become really clean and pure and holy," she said.

Sister Mary Pat threw her arms around her. "Patsy, I just know the Lord is going to do something special for you. He's got a beautiful plan for your life, and I'm anxious to see how He is going to control your future!"

I started laughing. "I do believe this is the craziest thing that ever happened to me!"

The other two joined in the laughter, and then Sister Mary Pat said, "Marji, you're something else. This is the oddest idea I've ever heard of. But let's hope it works."

"It's got to work!" Patsy said. And we all became very serious as we remembered the gravity of the situation that was calling for such unusual tactics.

Patsy and I moved toward the door, almost afraid to breathe. Just as I was about to open the door, I looked at her and gasped, "Oh, no! You forgot the sunglasses! Quick! Put on the sunglasses! No, Sister Mary Pat, you've got to keep out of sight!"

Patsy finally got the sunglasses on, and she looked almost exactly like Sister Mary Pat. I got the feeling my idea was going to work. We would soon know.

I slowly opened the door and looked across the street. Benny was still there, leaning up against the wall.

I whispered to Patsy, "Now whatever you do, don't say a word. Benny will probably taunt us. But don't say anything. Your voice will give us away!"

She nodded.

Sure enough, as soon as Benny saw us, he yelled, "Hey, preacher lady, did you win another soul?"

"Benny, you'd better keep your mouth to yourself," I shouted back. "God's going to get you yet!"

I should have left well enough alone, for my comments apparently upset him, and he headed toward us.

I grabbed Patsy's arm. "Run for your life!" I commanded, and I meant exactly what I said.

We took off, Patsy's robe flying in the wind. Fortunately Benny had to dodge some traffic to get across the street, so we got a little start on him.

Up ahead I saw a group of about five construction workers. I ran up to them and said, "Gentlemen, I need your help."

"And what do you and Sister need?"

"There's this guy down the street who is chasing us. When he comes by here, could you just delay him a little?"

"You mean that big brute headed this way?" one asked as he pointed toward Benny.

"That's the guy."

"Hey, listen, no problem. No problem. We'd be glad to help you and especially to help Sister there."

We took off again, but halfway down the block I just had to turn and see what happened. Just as Benny got near the men, one of them took a shovel and stuck it between Benny's feet. Benny went tumbling into the gutter.

I yelled, "Praise the Lord!"

The construction workers looked up the street at me. Then they looked at Benny and laughed. I knew he would be mad, but I also knew he wasn't likely to take on all five of them!

Patsy saw Benny sprawled in the gutter. "I sure don't understand this, Marji. I don't know whether it was the prayers or the quick thinking of those construction workers. But whatever happened, someone must be on my side!''

I wanted to savor that view of Benny in the gutter, but I knew we needed every minute we had. I grabbed Patsy's arm again, and we took off, running.

As we turned a corner, I spied Sister Mary Pat just ahead.

''I saw Benny take off after you,'' she said, ''so I went around the other way. Are you all right?''

''So far. Let's find a place for a quick change of clothing, and we'll be on our way up to the Walter Hoving Home.''

''I don't think we'd better,'' Sister Mary Pat said. ''What about Benny? Suppose he were to come running around that corner and spotted Patsy?''

She was right. Just because we had gotten out of the counseling center didn't mean we were safe yet.

''Are you sure you don't mind if we keep your clothes a little while longer, then?''

Sister Mary Pat smiled. ''Go ahead and keep them. I have more back at my apartment.''

''That's what I like about you, Sister; you're always so giving and generous.''

''No, not really,'' she said. The whole idea wasn't offending her now.

Out of the corner of my eye I saw Benny Barnes turn the corner. He was limping, but he still had fire in his eyes.

The other two saw him about the same time I did. I grabbed Patsy's arm, and we ran one way. Sister Mary Pat took off in another direction.

Then something happened that I should have anticipated, but hadn't. Benny didn't start chasing us. He started after Sister Mary Pat. He thought she was Patsy! Maybe our disguise had been all too successful!

Patsy and I were soon in the subway, headed for Grand Central Station. But I kept wondering about Sister Mary Pat. Would Benny catch up with her? Maybe she could outrun him when he was limping. If he caught her, would he kill her, thinking she was Patsy? Or would he kill her anyway, because she had helped us trick him? Had I sacrificed one life to save another?

What would happen to Sister Mary Pat? It would be some time before I found out. But at least for now we were safely on our way to Garrison.

11

It was about ninety minutes, by train, up to Garrison. I went into a small store and called the Walter Hoving Home. In just a few minutes, one of their staff picked us up.

I was overwhelmed as we entered the grounds of the home, a beautiful thirty-seven-acre estate. I was used to attractive homes, but I guess I just wasn't expecting this kind of home to be so beautiful. What a lovely place for these girls to learn more about Jesus.

The main home on the grounds is a large three-story English Tudor mansion. I learned later that the property also contains other homes at which the girls stay.

I think the Bentons were a little surprised when I arrived with what they at first thought was a nun seeking admission to the home! But when I explained the situation with Patsy and, how, because of her pimp, we had to spirit her out of the city, the home immediately took her in. Patsy was now safe and secure.

I spent some time with the Bentons, looking over their program. Reverend Benton told me that whenever I needed to send a girl, they would be more than happy to help me out. I was so pleased. I thought that's the way it would be; and, sure enough, it was. It made me more determined than ever to go back to the Lower East Side and try to rescue as many girls as possible and send them up here to this beautiful place.

Of course, they wanted to show me around the

grounds, too. The home has acres and acres of green grass and trees and a couple of horses. They have a swimming pool that is fed naturally by a stream that runs through the property.

It was such a contrast to our concrete jungle. It was so peaceful, so restful. But most of all, everywhere I sensed the presence of the Lord. God was certainly in this place.

Later that day, when I got back to the apartment, I found Uncle Alex and Aunt Amilda were quite worried about me. In the excitement, I had forgotten to tell them where I was going. Uncle Alex seemed especially fretful that I wasn't at the counseling center at five, for him to walk me home. I guess he thought that Luigi or Benny had finally caught up with me.

After I explained my mission of mercy, they both seemed happy that it was successful. You should have heard Uncle Alex laugh at the scheme we had pulled on Benny Barnes. I hoped that his interest was a beginning—that God was working in a subtle way in his heart. Maybe it wouldn't be long now until he would give his heart to Jesus. Wouldn't that be a miracle?

The following day I plunged back into my activity. I intended to go by and check with Sister Mary Pat to see how she had made out, getting away from Benny, but I got so busy that it just slipped my mind. I had more people come by than usual. I guess people were finding out about how I helped Patsy. So people dropped in about problems with jobs, rent, bills, landlords. I know I'm not too professional about all these problems, but they seemed to appreciate someone who would listen to them. It also gave me a good opportunity to share how Jesus could help them and give them grace to overcome their problems. Of course, where I could, I offered some direct aid. In fact, I took time to go to the unemployment agency with one girl. I knew that if all they got from me was a sermon, they probably wouldn't listen.

I could hardly believe it was five o'clock so soon, and I started putting my things away, looking for Uncle Alex. But he didn't come. That concerned me, because I really wasn't anxious to walk home alone tonight—especially after what we had done to Benny yesterday.

When Alex didn't come for what seemed a long time, I decided I'd better chance it. I didn't want to wait until after dark.

I locked the door and started toward the apartment. About a block down the street, I saw Aunt Amilda coming toward me, all out of breath.

Oh, no! I thought. *Something's happened to Uncle Alex! He's had a heart attack or . . . .*

She tried to tell me, as she caught her breath. "I'm so sorry about Uncle Alex not being down here to meet you tonight, Marji, but the police just came and hauled him away."

"Hauled him away? Whatever happened?"

"Oh, Marji, I just don't know what to make of this one. He's been accused of raping a little girl!"

Aunt Amilda's face was white as a sheet, and her eyes were brimming with tears.

I just couldn't believe Uncle Alex would do something like that. I knew he drank a lot, but I could never imagine him getting involved in a terrible thing like rape.

Amilda was looking to me for reassurance. "Marji, you don't believe your uncle would do something like that, do you?"

"Of course not. He just doesn't seem the type."

And then I thought: Sometimes it's those we don't think are the type who do these things. But certainly not Uncle Alex. Or would he? It seemed highly unlikely.

"I am sure this is a case of mistaken identity, Aunt Amilda. I just can't think it would be Uncle Alex."

"Oh, Marji, you should have been there when the police came. As soon as they told Alex what they were booking him for, they read him his rights. He went absolutely berserk."

"Well, I suppose if he is innocent, he probably would have had a bad reaction to being arrested."

"Marji, it was awful," she sobbed. "As soon as the officers started toward him, he ran to the kitchen and pulled out a butcher knife and started waving it around. The next thing I knew, an officer whipped out his revolver and yelled for Alex to drop the knife, or he'd blow his brains out. Poor Alex. He finally dropped the knife, and they handcuffed him and led him away.

"He was screaming, Marji. And do you know what he was screaming? 'Please, please, don't take me now. I've got to go down to the counseling center and pick up my niece!' "

"You're kidding!"

"No, no! In fact, he begged and pleaded for them to let him go for just three minutes, and he would run down and get you and bring you back, and then they could take him to the police station. Of course, the officers wouldn't hear of it. All the way out to the police car he was screaming, 'Please! Please! Please let me get my niece!' It was so sad! Marji, I think he was more concerned about your getting home safe than he was about the charge. He really cares about you!''

I now knew beyond a shadow of a doubt that God was working in my uncle's heart.

''Aunt Amilda, we must go down to the police precinct. Maybe we can post bail or something.''

''Oh, Marji, the officer said to bring some kind of identification with me. I mentioned you to one of the officers, because Alex was yelling your name. I told him what you were doing. He said for you to bring down some type of certification that you have a counseling center. I don't suppose you have a license or anything, do you?''

''No, I haven't gotten into that type of counseling. But I'm sure there is something at the office I could take down to show the officers. Let's see. I have some correspondence addressed to me. And I have some rent slips.''

''Well, get anything you can.''

''I know what I can bring. The Carlsons had me sign a lease agreement, and it is made out to the counseling center. That should be proof enough. I'll bring that.''

''Good! You go back and get those things, and I'll go on to the apartment to get some extra money. I've got a little saved up that Alex doesn't know about. Maybe it will help us with the bail.''

We set off in opposite directions.

Back at the center, I unlocked the door, walked

quickly to my desk, and reached for the drawer.

Just as I opened the drawer, it happened. I don't know if I can really explain it, but I saw a blinding flash and heard a loud boom.

The next thing I knew, I was out lying on the street. My face hurt. I reached up and touched it. I was bleeding profusely.

I couldn't get up, but I could see that the front window and front wall of the counseling center were completely gone. I immediately suspected what had happened. Someone had planted a bomb!

I was in shock. My left arm was all out of shape. I decided it probably was broken. At least it was there.

The crowd gathered almost immediately. I remember hearing Aunt Amilda screaming. And someone yelled, "Who would do a thing like this?"

I figured I knew. It had to be either Benny Barnes or Luigi Columbo. So this was their way of getting rid of me! It was probably Benny, because I had helped Patsy. He was going to be sure I didn't mess with any of his other girls.

In moments the police were on the scene, and then the ambulance arrived. That's the last I remember.

When I woke up, I was lying in clean sheets in a hospital bed, looking into the very concerned face of my father. Tears glistened on his cheeks, and I heard him say over and over, "I knew we shouldn't have let her get involved in this kind of thing. I knew it! I knew it!"

I tried to reach out toward him, but my hands wouldn't move. Was I paralyzed? Then I noticed Mom standing there. When she saw my eyes open, she stooped and kissed me.

"Oh, my little darling, we thought we had lost you," Dad said. "But the doctors were able to pull you through."

"Thank God," I murmured. "I . . . I . . . I . . , I . . . I . . ."

Then I felt myself fading again.

The next time I came to, the room was dark. No one was there.

I could remember a little of what had happened. And now I was wondering just how badly I was hurt. Had I lost any arms or legs?

With great effort I lifted my head ever so slightly. It looked as if my feet and arms were all there. My left arm was in a cast. Yes, I knew it was broken. I could feel heavy bandages all over my body.

Then I felt the pain! You can't imagine! Every bone in my body cried out. Pain jabbed my side. I must have let out a cry, because a nurse came running. When she looked at me, I managed a weak smile.

"Oh, wonderful!" she exclaimed.

I didn't feel very wonderful.

"I need to tell the supervisor!" And she was gone.

The next thing I remember was the supervisor bending over me and asking, "How are you doing?"

Very weakly I responded, "Thank God, I'm alive."

"You certainly can thank God, young lady. We thought we had lost you again. Here, let me give you something for your pain."

Just then Mom and Dad came in again. I mumbled something to them, but I was too weak to try to talk. I remember Dad trying to ask me who could have done this to me and the nurse telling him I needed to rest now. I tried to think, but I couldn't concentrate on anything for very long, and I guess I must have drifted off again.

The next morning, when my folks returned, I said, "Hi!" as they came through the door. You should have seen their excitement. They both nearly pounced on me and kissed me. They were both talking at once.

Dad fell on his knees beside the bed. "Oh, Marji, it is so good to hear your voice. We didn't know if you were going to make it last night."

I tried to reach out and touch my dad, but I was too weak to move.

After a few minutes he got started in on what had been bothering him so much: "Marji, the police are investigating the bombing. They still don't have any leads. Did you have any enemies?"

Did I dare tell my father about Luigi Columbo and Benny Barnes? That might upset him so much that he would never let me go back to the counseling center again! So all I said was, "Well, Dad, I've had some opposition. But I know that God has everything under control."

"What do you mean, you had opposition? Who?" Dad angrily demanded.

I just stared at the ceiling.

"Marji! I've got to know!"

"Dad, I honestly don't know who bombed the counseling center, but I've had a few problems."

"What kind of problems?"

Dad was getting so furious that a nurse came in and told him he would have to be quiet. I know she was afraid he was upsetting me.

"Dad, sit down," I said. "I want you to take this calmly. My counseling center is located next door to a pornography shop, and the guy who owns it, Luigi Columbo, has made threats. Also, just yesterday I rescued a girl from her pimp. The pimp's name is Benny Barnes. He has made threats, too. Now, Dad, I honestly don't know if these guys did it, but they would be my two top suspects.''

"That's all I need," Dad said, as he jumped up again. "I'll have the police on those two guys right away. If either of them did it, we're soon going to find out!''

He bent over and kissed me; then he stormed out of the room. I knew he would turn his hurt over me into vengeance toward others. That wasn't what the Bible taught. But I also knew it would be useless for me to try to stop him.

Mom stayed close to me all day. That evening Bucky and Aunt Amilda came.

I asked about Uncle Alex. She said he had been released that morning. He was in the police lineup, and the victim didn't pick out Alex. The girl admitted it was a case of mistaken identity, and he was freed. They even dropped the resisting arrest charge, because of the circumstances.

Amilda told me Alex had wanted to come, but he was so embarrassed over the charges of rape that he just couldn't face me. I figured it was more likely that he was afraid he would see my father.

I could understand that. Uncle Alex was making good progress. But he probably really wasn't ready to see my dad yet.

As I slowly improved, the police would spend a little more time each day questioning me. They told me they had picked up both Luigi and Benny but had to release them because there was absolutely no evidence to link them to the crime. Both of them had airtight alibis. Naturally they would; they were both smart operators.

My father was almost out of his mind, trying to track down the person who planted that bomb. The experts decided it had been planted in a drawer of my desk and that it was a time bomb.

I guess by this time I really suspected Luigi. I knew that his business had suffered since I had opened up the counseling center. And when a man like Luigi gets desperate, he'll stoop to anything. I had been gone for a short time that afternoon. He could easily have known that.

But what about Benny Barnes? No one crossed him, he said. But I had crossed him in rescuing Patsy.

As I improved, they allowed me to have more visitors. It was so wonderful to see people from the neighborhood, especially those I had been able to help.

I still hoped Uncle Alex would come. But Aunt Amilda always had the same excuse for him.

I was in the hospital for two months. Fortunately I wasn't paralyzed. I did have a few broken bones, but I began to mend quickly.

Mom and Dad insisted I come back to their home when I got out of the hospital. But I felt I needed to get back to my mission on the Lower East Side just as soon as I could. Aunt Amilda said she would take good care of me. So my folks finally consented.

That was a happy day for me. Whoever bombed me out was going to be in for a big surprise. They couldn't get rid of me that way! But I wondered what changes might have taken place in the two months I was in the hospital.

12

After those two months, when I was finally released from the hospital, Aunt Amilda came in a taxi to get me. On the way back, she told the driver to go by the counseling center. I guess she thought I'd like to see what it looked like and how miraculous it was that I had survived.

But when we pulled up in front of the center, I couldn't believe my eyes. Instead of looking at a bombed-out hulk, I noticed that the building had a new front on it. And a huge sign hung across the front window: WELCOME HOME, MARJI!

Once again I felt tears coming, but these were tears of joy. "Oh, Aunt Amilda! How wonderful! How wonderful! But who would do all this?"

"Well," she explained, "some of your friends got together. You'd be surprised, Marji, at how many friends you have down here—friends that we didn't even know about. You have really won the hearts of a lot of people who just can't get over your love and concern for them!

"Some of the merchants donated money for the work. We got some supplies free. And several carpenters came by after hours and fixed it all up. Wait till you see inside. It looks absolutely beautiful!"

She was right. It looked so pretty. I inhaled the wonderful, clean smell of new paint. All the furniture was new. And there was a new desk for me, and wall-to-wall carpet. Oh, it was absolutely thrilling.

As I looked around, all I could say was, "Praise the Lord! Praise the Lord!" Of course, I had to shed a few more tears, too!

I felt so warm inside. At times before I had felt all alone down here on the Lower East Side. But I guess when you're down and out and need help, it's always surprising how God sends such wonderful friends to encourage you. I loved Him so much for knowing just what I needed!

As Aunt Amilda and I stood there, people began to walk in. I recognized most of them—people I had helped in some small way and their friends and relatives.

One of the ladies brought a cake. Someone brought coffee. And before long the counseling center was filled with people for the welcome-home party they had so lovingly planned for me.

It all so overwhelmed me that I choked to try to keep back the tears. I just couldn't believe what was happening. These people were so wonderful. And it became obvious that God was turning something that someone had meant for evil into something good for me and for His purposes in the Lower East Side!

Just a few weeks earlier, as I had lain in a hospital bed, I had really wondered if I should come back here. Maybe the people really didn't care. Maybe my counseling center would end up a burned-up hole, like a lot of other storefronts in the area. Maybe I was just what some of the people had called me—a religious do-gooder who wouldn't last. Or maybe I was a religious nut.

Now I felt so ashamed of myself for even entertaining those thoughts. All these wonderful people were really behind me and were concerned about the work. Praise the Lord!

I guess we must have stayed at the celebration for two hours. I would have stayed 'longer, but Aunt Amilda insisted that I must get to the apartment for some rest. "Remember, I promised your parents I'd take care of you," she said. "If you want to stay down here . . . ."

It didn't take any more reminding.

I had hoped that Uncle Alex would come by the counseling center to be a part of my welcome-home party, but he didn't. He was waiting for us at the apartment, though—drunk!

He was sitting in front of the TV, a beer can in his hand, unshaved, dirty. It was almost as if I was reliving those first moments when I had met him down here.

As we walked into the apartment, he laughed in that hollow, drunken laugh. "Hey, kid, you're lucky to be alive!"

"Yes, Uncle Alex. God was really watching out for me."

"God nothin'! It was just dumb luck!"

Something was very wrong! I had expected him to welcome me with open arms. But here he was drunk and with a terrible attitude, too!

Aunt Amilda insisted I go right to bed, because I was physically drained by now. So I got into my pajamas, rolled onto my cot, and immediately fell asleep. I guess I really needed the rest, because it was the next day when I awoke.

I had more visitors. Some even brought food. They were so concerned about me; I couldn't get over it.

I still wasn't well enough to start keeping hours at the center. In fact, I stayed in bed quite a bit of the time. That's probably the reason why, one night, I wasn't sleeping too well. I had just turned over and looked at my alarm. I remember it well; the numbers had just flicked from 1:59 to 2:00. I closed my eyes to try to go back to sleep, when I heard my bedroom door creak. Then it slowly opened. Probably Aunt Amilda checking on me, I told myself. She had been so solicitous of my welfare—as if she was afraid that if she didn't take perfect care of me, my folks would take me away from her.

But as the door opened wider, I could make out the form of my uncle Alex. Why would he be sneaking into my bedroom in the middle of the night? Was he drunk again?

I decided to close my eyes and stay motionless.

His footsteps moved closer. I held my breath. He wouldn't attack me, would he? After all I had been through with the bombing and all, something terrible like that wouldn't happen to me, would it?

I could hear his heavy breathing. I sensed his face was close to mine. Was he on his knees? I inhaled quietly. No, there was no liquor on his breath. Maybe he was at least in control of his senses.

My heart beat wildly. What did he have in mind?

It seemed like an eternity of silence. Then I heard his muffled sobs.

I opened my eyes. Through the light of a neon sign outside my window, I could make out his form. Yes, he was kneeling beside my bed. His head was buried in the covers next to me. And he was weeping uncontrollably, but softly.

I slowly drew an arm out from under the covers and gently laid it across his back.

"Uncle Alex, what's the matter?"

He looked up at me, and his bottom lip quivered, just like a child trying to admit something. Then he put his head back down on the bed and sobbed.

I gently rubbed his back. Whatever he was trying to say, evidently he had decided to leave it unsaid. Maybe his conscience was bothering him about something.

He finally looked at me again. "Marji, I've got something terrible to tell you. I don't know if I can get this out, but I've come to confess to you a terrible thing that I have done."

Was he ready to admit that he had raped that girl? He probably thought he could confide in me and wanted me to know his side of the story. But why at two in the morning?

"Yes?"

His lips quivered again. "Marji, I don't know how to tell you this, but I do so hope that you will understand. But . . . but . . . but . . . but. . . ."

He broke down again.

Finally he raised his head and looked away from me. That's when he blurted it out: "I'm the one who planted that bomb down at your counseling center!"

I was fully awake now! I couldn't believe what I was hearing. Did he say what I thought he had said?

I pushed myself across the bed, up against the wall, and flipped on the light. Alex threw his head down on

the covers and wept. I don't think I've ever seen anyone cry like that.

But I wasn't feeling sorry for him. My first reaction
was total anger. This dirty, good-for-nothing drunk,
who was getting support from my father, had tried to
kill me!

He kept crying, and I didn't do anything to try to
comfort him.

Finally he raised his head. "Marji," he said, "you
must believe that I honestly didn't try to kill you.
Please listen to what I have to say. Then I'll let you be
the judge."

I was so angry; I didn't know what to think.

"Marji, I know you're a good Christian and a very
wonderful person. I've been hoping that somehow you
could help me to be reconciled with my brother. For
years now I've struggled in poverty and filth down
here on the Lower East Side. I know I was wrong
when I came here, but I came here because I wanted to
hurt Harry. It really hasn't worked. I'm the one who
has been hurt by it. I have a terrible problem with
alcohol, and it's a living hell. My anger is destroying
me. I really wanted out."

I began to realize something of the torment this man
was living with, and I saw more clearly the horrible
consequences he was paying for his hatred and stub-
bornness. His waywardness was hurting him more
than anyone else.

"Marji," he went on, "when you came down here, I
couldn't imagine Harry letting you come. I figured he
must be out of his mind. I wouldn't have let my daughter do it.

"But for many weeks now I've watched you. I

didn't see how you could possibly make it here. But things happened. I had to admire the way you stayed with it. You really did care about the people down here. It really made me wonder about becoming a Christian like you, but I knew it was too late for me."

I started to interrupt, but I decided I had better let him go on. I knew that God had been working in his heart. But why had Alex planted that bomb?

"I figured that maybe through you I would be reconciled with my brother. But then when you started getting threats, I worried that if something happened to you, that would be the end of any reconciliation hopes. I knew about Luigi and Benny. We talked about them. Remember when I tried to get you to leave, and you wouldn't? And that thing you pulled with Sister Mary Pat had the whole community laughing at Benny Barnes. I knew he would try to get you for that.

"Anyway, that's when I got the idea of planting the bomb. If it destroyed your counseling center, then you would have to leave, and you wouldn't get killed."

"But, Uncle Alex, don't you know that I almost died? If you didn't want me to die, why did you plant the bomb? And if I had been killed, you would have ended up in the penitentiary for life. Don't you understand that?"

"Marji! Marji! Marji! Please, please, try to understand! I didn't try to kill you! In fact, I had set the bomb to go off at five-thirty that evening, knowing you would be safely out of the building by that time.

"And then, just by a quirk of circumstances, the police came and arrested me on those false charges of raping that girl. It was absolutely ridiculous. I never raped anybody.

"I tried to get the police to let me go down and get you. I screamed and hollered and begged, but it didn't do any good. I had planned to get you at five, just as I always did, so you wouldn't have been there when the bomb went off. But at five-thirty I was down at the police station, going out of my mind. I couldn't tell them I had planted a bomb. I was just hoping that you had left and that everything had gone according to the way I had planned it."

So that was it. What he was telling me squared with what Aunt Amilda had said. Uncle Alex really hadn't tried to kill me; he only wanted to scare me. But his plans got fouled up.

"Marji," he continued, "you can't imagine how relieved I was when I learned that you were going to make it. I would never have been able to forgive myself if you had died. In fact, while they were worried about whether or not you were going to pull through, I had already decided to kill myself if you died. I just couldn't have faced that!"

He buried his head in the covers and sobbed again. And over and over he mumbled, "Thank You, God, that Marji is still alive. Thank You that Marji is still alive."

I really believe he was sincere. All the facts were somehow fitting together now.

As he slowly raised his head again, he said, "Marji, I don't know if you believe me, but what I've told you is the honest-to-God truth. I told you the truth. I really did, Marji. And, if somehow you believe me, would you please forgive me? I didn't want to hurt you. You are my darling niece. I even think I would give my own life to spare you. Oh, Marji! Marji! I didn't want to kill you or hurt you. Please! Please! Can you possibly forgive me?''

By now I was feeling so sorry for him. Yes, I believed what he was telling me. ''Of course, Uncle Alex, I forgive you.''

That word *forgive* brought another flood of tears from him. Then he blurted out, ''Marji, there's something else. I feel so ashamed because of what I did. I know you believe God. Could you do me a favor and say a little prayer for me? This whole thing has made me know that I need God. I know I really don't deserve Him, but maybe if you pray for me, He'll hear you.''

I knew this was no time to argue theology. Of course, God would hear Uncle Alex's prayer. But right now what he really needed was for somebody to pray for him. I moved over next to him, put my arm around his shoulder, and began to pray.

The next thing I knew, this is what I heard from my uncle: ''Lord Jesus, I'm a dirty, rotten, filthy sinner. I've made a terrible mess of my life, and I'm so ashamed and guilty. Please forgive me for all my sins and make me into a new person in You. I confess all my sins to You, and I want to be a Christian who will please You. Please take me now.''

I slapped him on the back. ''Uncle Alex, do you know what you just did?''

He looked at me, a big smile filtering across his face.

''Uncle Alex, you just prayed and asked Jesus to come into your heart. You asked Him to be your Saviour. You've become a Christian!''

''Well, Marji, that's what I wanted to do. Do you think He will listen to me? Do you think it will work?''

''Do I think it will work? Oh, Uncle Alex! It has

already worked! Jesus has just forgiven all your sins, because you asked Him to!"

His smile grew even bigger. "Well, I'll be! I'm a Christian! I know it!"

"Aunt Amilda, come here!" I yelled.

In seconds she rushed into my bedroom, rubbing the sleep from her eyes. When she saw Alex kneeling on the floor by my bed, she yelled, "What is going on here? Alex, what are you doing in Marji's bedroom at this hour of the night?"

"Aunt Amilda, sit down!" I commanded. "We've got some great news!"

She walked over and sat on the bed beside me.

"Uncle Alex just became a Christian! He just received Jesus as his Saviour!"

Amilda jumped up. "Alex! Alex! Is it really true? Is it really true?"

"Yes, my dear. It's really true."

He was off his knees now, and they were embracing as if they had just discovered how wonderful each other was.

"Oh, Alex, if you become just one-tenth of the Christian that Marji is, you'll be the most lovable husband in the world. Oh, I'm so happy for you!"

I joined them in the hugging and crying. It was one of the happiest moments I could ever remember.

A few minutes later Alex guided Amilda to the side of my bed and sat there with her. "What about you, dear? Wouldn't you like to be a Christian, too?"

She looked at me, and she looked back at him. "Oh, yes, Alex—more than anything else. I've wanted to for so long, but I've been waiting for you to make the first move."

"Well," he said, "it's not all that hard. If I remember right, all you have to do is to ask Jesus to forgive you and tell Him you're sorry for your sins. And then you just tell Him you'll live for Him. I guess that's all. Isn't that right, Marji?''

I nodded. Uncle Alex hadn't been a Christian for ten minutes, and already he was winning another person to the Lord!

We all bowed our heads as Amilda asked Jesus to forgive her sins. By faith she received Him into her heart. She, too, had been born again.

By now, of course, nobody was sleepy. So I started telling them a little of what it means to be a Christian. I pointed out that they needed to read the Bible and pray every day. And that they needed to tell other people what Jesus had done for them and to associate with other Christians in a church.

They drank in every word. They were so excited, so full of joy, so vibrant!

We lost all track of time, but the first few glimmers of daylight brought us back to reality. As they started to leave my bedroom, Alex turned to me and said, ''Marji, I'll explain to your aunt what happened. I'll have to ask her to forgive me, too. Please pray that she will understand.''

Amilda looked at me wonderingly, but I didn't say a word. This was something Uncle Alex was going to have to handle. I knew it would be tough for him. But I also knew that somehow God would help him. And I knew that Aunt Amilda, as a new Christian, was going to need to learn to forgive.

I eased back into my cot, exhausted, but I still couldn't sleep. I had been so excited about Uncle Alex's conversion that I had overlooked some obvious problems that now faced me because of his confession.

My dad hadn't let up one iota in trying to find the bomber and bring him to justice. What would he say when he found out it was his own brother?

Would Dad be so full of revenge that he would want Uncle Alex put in prison? If that happened, would Alex be strong enough to live a Christian life there?

13

My father had hired detectives to solve the bombing. Even if I didn't tell on Uncle Alex, suppose they learned that he had done it? That would end any hopes of a reconciliation. I wondered if the chances were gone now, anyway.

But I just couldn't see Uncle Alex going to jail, especially now that he had become a Christian. Oh, I knew that he probably would be able to be a Christian in prison. Other people had done that: Charles Colson had. But was Uncle Alex strong enough to withstand the pressures of being in prison? Probably not yet.

I spent the next several days thinking about the problem and praying about it. Somehow I felt that the solution might come if I could get Dad and Uncle Alex together, down at the counseling center.

The next day I phoned my dad at the office. He was always so thrilled whenever I called. We talked for a while, and then he got on the subject that seemed to possess him these days: "So help me, Marji, I just can't figure out who bombed your counseling center. The police department has some of its best men on the case, and I've hired some private detectives. They've interviewed thousands of people, but there is no strong clue. Both Benny Barnes and Luigi Columbo have come up clean. Can you think of anyone else who might have done it?"

My heart beat wildly. I just couldn't blurt out over the telephone that it was Uncle Alex, or Dad would have the whole New York City Police Department converging on our apartment. But I had to tell him something, before he found out anyway.

"Dad, I think I might have some more information, but I don't want to discuss it on the phone."

"Yeah, I know," he cut in. "Maybe your phones are tapped."

That was easy!

"Dad, why don't you meet me tomorrow morning at ten at my counseling center? I want you to see what the people have done to fix it up for me. And then I can talk to you, too."

"Hey, that sounds great, honey. I hope we're getting closer to solving this case. I tell you, Marji; as soon as we nab this guy, I'm going to personally see that he gets a hundred years in the slammer!"

I gulped. "Dad, let's not be too hard. You know we have to be Christian about all this."

"I don't know what you mean by that. But it seems I remember something in the Bible about an eye for an eye. I'll go with that. Nobody is going to try to kill my daughter and get away with it!"

He was getting so upset that I knew it was pointless to try to discuss the matter further. When Dad made up his mind, almost nothing could change it.

"See you tomorrow at ten then?"

"Okay, honey. Should I bring my detectives?"

"Oh, no, Dad! Don't do that! That would spoil everything! Just come yourself in a taxi. Nobody else. Promise?"

Well, Dad was coming. Alone, I hoped. But my next

problem was Alex. Would he go along with it?

At lunch I told Alex and Amilda why I had called my father. I waited for Uncle Alex's answer.

He pushed back his plate and replied very deliberately, "Marji, I know I have done wrong, and I am willing, now, to take any consequences. Your aunt and I have discussed this at great length these past few days. If I have to go to prison, then I have to go to prison. I have done wrong, very wrong, and I am willing to take my punishment."

I wanted to cry! Somehow I just couldn't bring myself to have Uncle Alex wind up in prison. There had been such peace and love in their little apartment these past few days, since Alex and Amilda had found Jesus as their Saviour.

I suggested we pray and commit the whole matter to the Lord. They agreed. Uncle Alex said he was certainly willing to do whatever the Lord wanted him to do and that he would go to the center with me tomorrow morning.

Aunt Amilda broke down and started weeping. I put my arms around her and cried, too. Somehow God had to undertake this problem.

I hadn't been down to the center since my welcome-home party, and I decided this would be a good time to go. I wanted to be sure everything was ready for that meeting tomorrow.

As I walked to the center, I saw again how beautiful it was, and I marveled at the love that had brought it back from ruins.

Before I realized what I was doing, I caught myself

glancing across the street to see if Benny Barnes was there. Of course, he wasn't. But that reminded me of something else. In all those people the other day, why wasn't Sister Mary Pat at the center?

I hadn't seen her since we had rescued Patsy. She was in Patsy's clothes, and Benny had been chasing her, thinking she was Patsy.

Strange that she wasn't at the welcome-home party. Or that nobody mentioned that she'd helped to clean the place up. What had happened to her?

Maybe Benny Barnes got her. Maybe her body had been dumped in some deserted alley or thrown into the river. Maybe my friends were so concerned about my recovery that they didn't want to shake me with tragic news.

Suddenly I just had to know what happened to Sister Mary Pat. The counseling center could wait.

I walked the four blocks to the Saint Thomas Church. I couldn't move as fast as the last time I went down there. But as I walked, wild thoughts entered my mind. What would I tell the people at the church? that I was part of a plan that had resulted in Sister Mary Pat's murder?

I shuddered. Could they arrest me for the plot that involved Benny Barnes and her? Would I end up in prison, too? I sensed I was in deep trouble.

I stopped. Maybe I wouldn't say anything. But I knew that wouldn't be right. So I continued toward the church, my feet sort of dragging on the way.

Even so, it wasn't long until I stood before the church. This time I headed straight for the side door. But it was locked. I couldn't get inside!

I knocked—no answer. I knocked louder—still no answer.

"Oh, God, please send someone to open this door!"

I knocked again—still no answer.

Disappointed and frustrated, I turned to walk away. Just then I heard the door creak. I turned and stared in disbelief. There stood a smiling Sister Mary Pat!

I ran over and threw my arms around her. "Oh, Sister Mary Pat! You're alive! Alive! Praise the Lord!"

She looked at me kind of strangely. "Of course I'm alive. And so are you."

"What happened to you?" I asked. "Where have you been?"

"You haven't heard?"

"No. No one told me anything about you. I thought maybe Benny had killed you."

"No, I'm very much alive, as you can see. I guess you might say I've been on an extended vacation. I just got back."

"Vacation?"

"Yes," she laughed. "You might call it that. Come on in; I'll tell you all about it. You look as if you need to sit down."

When I was comfortably seated in her office, she said, "I guess I'd better start from the time I last saw you and Patsy. Remember? I was in Patsy's clothes."

"I'll never forget that."

"Well, Benny saw me and figured I was Patsy, I guess. He started chasing me. Suddenly I knew I was running for my life. Just then a car pulled up to the curb, and the guy motioned for me to jump in. It was broad daylight, so I did. I knew it was still a big chance, but . . . ."

"You mean you got into a car with a total stranger?"

"Well, what did you want me to do? keep running?"

"I guess you're right."

"Well, we drove for a few blocks. I was so terrified that I couldn't ask him to take me to the church. Besides, I don't think he would have believed I was a nun! So I just stared straight ahead. And the next thing I knew he had pulled into an alley. It was deserted. Then he slid over and put his arm around me."

I started laughing. I knew what he thought.

"Would you believe he handed me fifty bucks? He thought I was a prostitute!"

"Well, you were dressed like one."

"Marji," she lowered her voice to a whisper, "I guess I can trust you with my thoughts. As I looked at that fifty-dollar bill, I almost decided to grab it and run! I mean, that guy deserved to have his money taken from him. How dare he proposition a nun? I wanted to teach him a lesson."

I giggled. "Then what happened?"

"Well, I screamed and jumped out of the car, ran out to the street, and finally got back to the church.

"But you won't believe what happened the next day. Someone from our parish saw me getting into the car with that guy—and there I was, dressed in jeans. I don't even know the name of the man in the car, but I guess everybody on the street knows him. Apparently he's slept with every prostitute in the area. Well, the member of our church told the mother superior that I was out prostituting!"

The whole thing was so ridiculous that I was doubled over with laughter. She was laughing, too.

"Well, Marji, it wasn't funny at the time. Of course I denied prostituting. But I had to admit I did get into the car with that guy. Of course, the mother superior was flabbergasted that I would even do a thing like that. So I had to tell her why Patsy and I exchanged clothes. She really got upset over that. She told me I was never to do anything like that again.

"After she calmed down, I think she could see that we were able to save Patsy's life. But she told me she had to discipline me because I had broken the rules. She punished me by sending me up to Nova Scotia for three months."

"And that's what you meant by an 'extended vacation'?"

"Exactly."

"Well, Sister Mary Pat, I'm terribly sorry I caused you so much trouble. I really hated to ask you to do that, but I didn't know how else to get Patsy up to the Walter Hoving Home. And, by the way, she's doing fantastically up there. She's taken Jesus as her Saviour and is really into their program!"

"Wonderful. I think it all turned out well, Marji! My punishment wasn't all that bad. I enjoyed Nova Scotia. But I had to promise the mother superior I would behave myself. No more exchanges of clothing."

"Well, Sister, that was probably a once-in-a-lifetime experience. It probably wouldn't work again, anyway! And I've had a few experiences since then, too."

"Yes, I heard about the bombing. They still haven't caught the bomber, have they? I imagine it was Benny, but no one will ever be able to prove it."

"No, it wasn't Benny. I know who did it, but I'm really in a jam over it."

"Whatever do you mean?"

"Well, this is in strict confidence: The person who

planted the bomb was my uncle Alex!''

"Alex Parker?" she shrieked.

"Please, hold it down!''

"You don't mean your *uncle* tried to kill you?"

I explained as best I could about my family—about the will and the problem between Uncle Alex and Dad. Then I explained that Alex really hadn't been trying to hurt me: He just wanted to frighten me into leaving the Lower East Side because he was still hoping that somehow I might be able to reconcile him and my father.

"But God used all this in an amazing way," I said.

"What way?"

"Well, after Uncle Alex confessed this to me, he and Aunt Amilda received Jesus as their Saviour. This crisis over the bombing brought them to a point of desperation, and now they have turned their lives over to the Lord. Isn't that beautiful?"

"Oh, praise the Lord!" Sister Mary Pat responded. "It is just absolutely amazing what good God can bring out of terrible circumstances. But I don't really see where you've got a problem."

"My problem is this. My dad has made a big case out of the bombing. He's determined to find and punish whoever did it, regardless of what it costs. He is coming to the counseling center at ten tomorrow morning, and I'm going to have to tell him. I know he'll go into orbit and will probably want to kill Uncle Alex. There'll be a big trial and all, and Alex may even go to prison. I don't know if I could take that."

"Marji, to tell you the truth, this really isn't that big a problem."

"What do you mean, it isn't a problem? There's no

big problem if my dad wants to kill Uncle Alex? no big problem if Uncle Alex has to go to jail? I don't think he's a strong enough Christian to face that. I say I've got one big problem!''

''Wait a minute. Let me tell you something. You can go to the police and tell them what happened. Then all you have to do is tell them that you're not going to press charges. If you don't press charges, they'll have to drop the whole thing.''

''You mean that if I don't press charges, that'll be the end of it?''

''Yes, it's happened before.''

It seemed too simple. I wondered if she really knew that much about the law.

''Are you really sure?'' I asked again.

''Marji, I know. It happened once here at the church. We had a break-in, and the person was finally caught. But he was a member of this church. We were in a dilemma. The person agreed to make restitution, and we didn't want to press charges. The officer told us if we didn't press charges, they couldn't do anything about it. So that was the end of the matter.''

I breathed a heavy sigh of relief. There was a way out!

I told Sister Mary Pat about the way the counseling center had been fixed up for me, and how thrilled I was at the response I was seeing in the neighborhood. I let her know that she and I were becoming sort of folk heroes for what we had pulled on Benny!

We had a lot of catching up to do, but I knew I needed to save my strength for tomorrow. She borrowed a parish car and drove me back to the apartment.

I spent a lot of time praying before I went to bed that night. I knew I needed extra help.

Uncle Alex was up early the next morning, praying and reading his Bible. It was such a thrill to see the change in his life!

At 9:45 he and I walked the two blocks to the counseling center. Aunt Amilda, bless her heart, had been there before us and had straightened everything up.

At 10:00 a cab pulled up in front, and my father came in the door of the center. He really didn't look around at things. He headed right for me and hugged me.

Then I led him into my office. He stopped abruptly. There sat Uncle Alex.

I held my breath. Would this work? Alex jumped up and stuck out his hand. "Henry, it's so good to see you again. Before you say one word, I've got something to say to you."

Dad stiffened. I knew he expected another tongue-lashing.

"Henry, will you please forgive me? For a number of years now, I've not been the person God wants me to be. I've been selfish, belligerent, and hateful concerning the will. I've tried to punish you for it in every way I could think of. Had I known what I know now, I would have taken it as God's will for my life. Harry, would you please forgive me for the way I've acted toward you? Would you please forgive me for being the lost sheep of the family?"

Dad stood there, blinking his eyes. I knew he couldn't believe what he was hearing.

"Dad, your brother is a new man now. He's not the same person you used to know. He's received Jesus

Christ as his personal Saviour. Jesus has made him into a loving, caring man."

Dad stood there, speechless.

Then Alex went over to him, embraced him, and began to sob. Dad was having a difficult time trying to handle it. I saw him bite his lower lip.

It was too much for me. I cry almost at the drop of a hat when I'm happy; so I started in, too. I guess that broke Dad up.

When he regained his composure, he said, "Alex, I just don't know what to make of all this. I certainly wasn't expecting anything like this when I came down here today. For many years I have dreaded meeting you, because I knew something of your condition. And now to see you happy like this is absolutely beyond belief! Of course, my brother, I forgive you."

"Praise the Lord!" I yelled. "Praise the Lord!"

After we were all sitting down, Dad said, "Marji, this is all absolutely wonderful. But when you asked me to come down here, you told me you had some information on the bombing. Naturally I'm anxious to hear that. I've got my men ready to move on it."

Alex glanced at me, and I glanced back. I felt my throat tighten. After this reconciliation, how could I possibly tell Dad what really had happened?

But I knew I had to do it. "Dad, now I want you to take it very easy. Please stay calm. The person who planted the bomb was Uncle Alex, but . . . ."

You should have seen my father explode! He jumped off the sofa and screamed, "Alex, there is absolutely no way you are going to get by with something like this! I knew what you said was too good to be true. You were just trying to butter me up, just playing a religious scheme to get on my good side. Well, I'm not falling for it! You've been a schemer ever since you were a kid. You would rather scheme than work. You schemed to get everything you could as a kid. But this time you've gone too far. Your scheming isn't going to get you out of this!"

Dad had his index finger almost touching Uncle Alex's nose. His other fist was clenched.

I waited for Uncle Alex to explode right back. He just wouldn't take anyone threatening him, I knew. But now he sat there, unmoved. God was really working in his life. This was another evidence of the change in him.

My father ranted and raved about how he was going to see Uncle Alex behind bars for this.

When he finally ran out of breath, I said, "Dad, I want you to sit down and let me tell you the rest of the story. It isn't as you imagine at all. Please sit down."

He looked at me, and he glared at Alex, but he slowly sat down.

"Dad, Uncle Alex didn't try to kill me. He only wanted to place a bomb in the counseling center, to frighten me so I would leave the Lower East Side. He was hoping that somehow I would be able to reconcile the two of you. He was scared that if I died—and I almost lost my life to Benny Barnes and Luigi Columbo—there would never be any chance of a reconciliation.

"He had intended to get me away from the center before the bomb went off. He always came to get me at five. But that night he was down at the police precinct, defending himself against a false charge of rape.

"You know the investigators found that the bomb

was set to go off at five-thirty. Uncle Alex always picked me up at five, and I would have been back at the apartment by five-thirty. But because of that false charge and the arrest, I had gone back to pick up some identification at the center, so I was there when the bomb went off. Please believe me. Uncle Alex didn't try to kill me.''

''Marji,'' Dad interrupted, ''you don't understand. We can't go by intentions. That bomb *did* go off. You *did* get blown out onto the street. You *did* almost die. And Alex *is* responsible. He is going to have to do time for this. No way am I going to let him get away with this nonsense!''

Uncle Alex still sat there silently. God was giving him such peace that I could hardly believe it.

''Dad, I want to tell you something else about this matter.''

''What's that?'' he snapped.

''I don't want to be disobedient or to disappoint you, but I've decided not to press charges against Uncle Alex.''

''Not press charges?'' Dad yelled. ''He is guilty, Marji! He must pay for what he has done!''

''That may be true, Dad, but I'm not going to press charges. I found out that if I don't press charges, nothing will happen.''

''Marji, I can't believe you. Don't you know that Alex almost killed you?''

''Dad, I know that. But I also know why. That's why I've decided just to commit this whole thing to the Lord and let Him take care of it.''

''Marji, I just cannot believe all this. Your uncle Alex is a schemer, and the tragic part of all this is that you're being duped by another of his schemes. Someday you'll grow up to face the truth. Believe me, I will have no part in any more of Alex's schemes!''

"Dad, please don't say that. I believe Uncle Alex really wants to serve the Lord. Please give him a chance, won't you?''

"Chance? Give him a chance? He's gotten second chances all his life. Well, this is the end. He's had his last chance!''

"Dad, don't say that. I know God has done something special in his life. I've seen evidence of it. You wouldn't want to hinder God, would you?''

Dad was so distraught that he let out an oath, something he hardly ever did when I was around. "I'm not the one who is hindering God,'' he yelled.

That finally brought Uncle Alex to his feet. I wondered what would happen now.

"Harry, you have every right to think that way,'' Alex said very calmly. "And I suppose if this had happened to me and my daughter, I would react the same way. I envy you for having a daughter like Marji. I'm trying to put myself in your position. You feel I need to be punished. I think you are right. I've done wrong. I'm sorry and ashamed of what I've done. Now I am ready to take my punishment. If you say I should pay for this and go to prison, then I'm ready to go now.''

Dad sat there dumbfounded.

"Dad, Uncle Alex and Aunt Amilda have already discussed the consequences. I didn't mention anything to Uncle Alex about not pressing charges. He came here today ready to go to prison!''

I let that sink in.

"But, Dad, do you really want your brother to go to prison? What about the publicity if that happens? The whole mess will be in the papers—everything you've tried to keep hidden all these years. They're going to dig into this for every juicy morsel they can find. What will that do to your business? What will it do to you and Mother and Bucky?''

That quieted him down in a hurry. I knew he hated the idea of bad publicity, of dirty family linen out before all the world. He buried his head in his hands, and for quite a while no one spoke.

Finally Dad got up, walked over, and threw his arms around me. "Marji, I just cannot believe all that has happened here this morning. I'm so torn between trying to believe Alex and you and my own feelings that I just don't know what to do.''

"I know it's hard to understand, Dad. We threw a couple of heavies at you today. You've been such a wonderful father to me in looking out for me. I know you feared for my life down here. I can understand that, and I appreciate it and love you for it. But, Dad, please, please believe Uncle Alex. It will mean so much to me if you do.''

He dropped his arms to his side. "Well, Marji, I guess I really don't have much choice, do I? I am trying to believe you. And it is very hard for me to suddenly start believing Alex. I just find it impossible to accept that something like this could happen to him.''

I smiled. "Somehow, somewhere, some place God is going to show you that what Uncle Alex has is real, Dad. I know he will be tempted to revert to his old ways. But I believe he is going to find out that the Lord will give him power to withstand every temptation.''

"I'll believe that when I see it!'' Dad said.

"Someday, Dad, you're going to be a believer!''

"Well, Marji, if this really works for Alex, you might

be surprised. Maybe I will become a believer.''

''Well, praise the Lord!'' Uncle Alex said.

''I've got to get back to the office, Marji. Further-more, I need time to think. I can't believe all that has happened here this morning.''

Dad turned and started to walk out. Then he came back and put his arm around my shoulder. ''I honestly don't understand all this. But there's one thing I'm so happy about, and that is that you're alive. I will say this: God has been good to me in sparing your life. Yes, He has been good.''

''Dad, that's not all. I'm still praying that someday you'll understand all that Christ wants to mean to you. He wants to be very special to you. You need Him.''

He released his grip around my shoulders and softly said, ''Maybe you're right.''

Uncle Alex and I walked down the street with Dad. Then he hailed a cab and drove away from our world.

Then Alex said, ''Marji, let's hurry and tell Amilda the news. I don't know what to say about your not pressing charges against me. That is so much more than I ever expected! I don't deserve it, but I'm so excited! I just can't get over your kindness to me!''

The next day I opened up the counseling center for business again. I felt as if a heavy burden had been rolled off my shoulders. Now I could get on with the work.

But as I sat there at my desk, rejoicing in how good God was to me, the door of the center flew open.

There stood a girl about my age, her hair terribly matted, her eyes glassy. She screamed, ''Can you help me?''

One look at her told me this was going to be a tough one!

14

"Hey, lady, I said, 'Can you help me?' "

Her voice was both desperate and demanding.

I walked from behind my desk. "Well, I don't know. What seems to be your problem?"

She was gritting her teeth; she was so terribly upset. I wondered what could be bugging her.

I admit that her approach sort of nettled me. How could I possibly know if I could help her if I didn't know what her problem was? But I controlled myself and tried to be as kind as possible.

"Well, for a number of months now I've been trying to help people around here. I know I can't solve all the problems, but I also know that no problem is too hard for the Lord. So let's talk about yours."

She flipped open her purse, jerked out a switch-blade, snapped it open, and started toward me.

Startled, I tried to jump back. But the only thing behind me was the wall. I started to grab a chair to protect myself with, but it was too late. She was already right up against me, her hand poised to strike.

"Don't do it!" I screamed. "Don't do it!"

Then she very deliberately put her arm down and laughed raucously. "You religious nuts are all the same. You talk about how wonderful it will be to go to heaven, but when you're almost there, you jump back and beg and plead, just like the rest of us sinners. And I really thought maybe *you* could help me!" Her voice

178

dripped with sarcasm as she shut her switchblade and slipped it back into her purse. She wheeled around and headed for the exit.

"Hey, now, wait just a minute!" I yelled after her. "You may think I'm a religious nut, but I am a human being. If someone were coming after you with a knife, wouldn't you jump back?"

She paused, her hand on the door handle. "Of course, you stupid nut. How many times you ever been stabbed? How many times you ever been cut? Believe me, it's excruciating pain! Of course I'd jump back!"

I smiled. "Now that's just what I'm talking about. I guess we're really kind of alike, aren't we?"

"What do you mean, alike? I'm a junkie who needs help, and you're a nice little Christian girl. I heard about you. People here on the Lower East Side are talking about that nice little Christian girl who has the counseling center. So I think maybe you can help me, and I come here to test you. And you flunk!"

"What did you expect me to do? Stand there and let you stab me?"

"I wasn't going to stab you, lady! I was just testing to see whether you're afraid. And you're a fraidycat."

I laughed. "As I told you, of course I'm scared. I'm human, too. But whether or not I'm afraid shouldn't be the measure of whether or not I can help you, should it? The reason I'm here is to try to help people. You want to talk about your problem?"

"Let's just forget it."

She started to open the door. But she was doing it so slowly that I sensed she really wasn't ready to go. I ran up to her and grabbed her arm. "Hey, wait a minute!

Let's at least talk about it. Maybe I can do something for you. We won't know, if we don't talk about it!"

"Naw, forget it. I don't think there's any hope for me, anyway."

"Oh, don't say that. Jesus specializes in helping impossible cases. He's the One who can help you, whatever your problem is."

She looked at me as if I had flipped. "Jesus? You kidding?"

She jerked loose. "I don't want to be no religious nut. I been in enough mental institutions for a lifetime!"

She was out the door now, and I followed her. I wasn't about to give up on this one!

"Where are you going?"

"None of your business."

"Well, wherever it is, I'm going with you."

"I'm going to get a cup of coffee."

"Great idea! It's time for my coffee break, anyway. I'll buy."

I was walking beside her now, but she wouldn't say another word. When we passed the coffee shop, she acted as if she were going to pass it by. I grabbed her arm again. Would she hit me? or knife me? Thank God, she didn't resist, and she rather meekly followed me into the coffee shop.

We found a booth at the back, where we could be alone, and ordered. I never could get used to the amount of sugar that junkies put in a cup of coffee!

For a few minutes she just sat there, sipping her coffee. I didn't push. Then she began to open up.

"Where did you start to go wrong?" I asked.

"Hey, before I tell you things like that, why don't

we introduce ourselves?''

I laughed. I guess sometimes I get in too much of a hurry. ''My name is Marji Parker. What's yours?''

''Cynthia Munson.''

''Well, I'm very happy to meet you, Cynthia. And I do hope my response to your switchblade hasn't turned you off.''

''Aw, not to worry. It was a stupid thing to do, anyway.''

''Well, I guess it is one way to test whether or not Christians are really anxious to go to heaven. Now take me. As somebody said, 'I'm ready to go, but I'm not rarin'!' ''

She laughed at that, and so did I. It broke the tension between us.

''Now, Cynthia, what can I do to help you?''

''Marji, it's like I said. I don't know if you can or if anybody can. I've been mixed up for so long now that I think I'm beyond help.''

''Now I don't want to sound religious to you. But let me say it again: No one is beyond the help of the Lord!''

''Well, let me tell you what happened, and you judge for yourself.''

I settled back to listen, as her story began to pour out. The rest of her coffee went untouched.

''Ever since I was a child, I've had problems with feelings of insecurity and loneliness. I mean, I would do anything to be accepted or approved. I wanted so much to be loved.

''Once when I was little, I stole some flowers from the neighbor's yard and brought them to my mother. I thought she would love me for that. Instead, she slapped me across the face and told me I was bad because I had stolen the flowers. Oh, Marji, she had no sympathy for me, no awareness that I was just trying to be accepted and loved. I've never forgotten that incident. Somehow it sort of became the pattern of my life.

"When no one, including my parents, gave me the love I craved, I figured there was something wrong with me. I kept trying to hide from other people.

"In my early teens, I thought that if I took drugs I would be accepted and be somebody—somebody worth loving. Of course, I was accepted by other people who took drugs; but as soon as the high wore off, we were all on our own. I was alone again.

"I got heavily into drugs, and then my parents started to pay attention to me. They realized they had a serious problem on their hands. Now you might not understand this part, but my parents are quite wealthy."

I smiled, but I didn't tell her why.

"They had their reputation to look out for, so they got me to a doctor. Would you believe he put me on tranquilizers? Of course, that only complicated the problem! It got so bad that they put me in a private hospital for six weeks. But when I got out, I went right back on drugs—the very day I got out!

"Then it was back to the hospital. This time, when I got out, they put me in a halfway house. I stayed a week.

"Well, Marji, it was a vicious circle. I went back to drugs, back to the hospital, back to the doctors, until finally I just gave up. I knew I could never survive the merry-go-round."

How many times had I heard a similar story? If only

somehow people would realize there was hope, for everyone, through Jesus.

But Cynthia wasn't through talking, and I didn't want to interrupt her.

"I eventually suffered a total break from reality. And this break began that endless journey in and out of mental institutions. You cannot believe the hell I went through. Marji, have you ever had a shock treatment?"

"No, but I suppose you had one?"

"One? I had thirty-two shock treatments! When that electricity hits you, it snaps back your head, and you go into unconsciousness. It was a hell that is difficult to describe. After thirty-two of them, I was becoming a vegetable!"

"You poor dear," I sympathized.

"Well, Marji, I'll tell you what really put the frosting on the cake. I'm sure there are good psychiatrists in mental hospitals, but the one I got really needed to be there as a patient, I think. You know what he finally told me? He said, 'Why should I waste my time on you? You are psychotic, and you always will be psychotic. There is just no hope for you.'

"Can you imagine, Marji, having someone say that to you? And I was in such bad shape that I started to believe him.

"Every time I saw that doctor, I started laughing like a crazy person. I guess maybe I *was* crazy. I had no rationale. I had accepted the fact that I was a vegetable and that the only happiness a vegetable would have would be to laugh.

"My folks finally arranged for my release. I think they realized I was getting no help there, and it was costing them a lot of money. They took me home, but I ran away to New York City. Three years ago I ended up here on the Lower East Side. I've done just about everything down here. I'm not very proud of myself." Her voice trailed off.

Now Cynthia had come to the end of her road. The Lower East Side was the last stop for many girls like her. The next step usually was suicide.

"Cynthia, would you believe that Jesus has been waiting all these years for you to turn your life over to Him?"

I saw tears start to trickle down her cheeks.

"Marji, I would do anything just to have peace of mind for two minutes. I mean anything. That's why I take drugs—to relieve my mind. I don't know what's the matter with me, but I guess I really am crazy. Just a crazy, good-for-nothing junkie."

I reached across the table, with a napkin, and gently wiped the tears from her cheeks.

She looked right into my eyes. "Marji, honestly now, is there any hope for me?"

"I'll stake my life on it, Cynthia."

Her eyes got wider. "Honest? I mean, real honest? You wouldn't lie to me, would you?"

"Cynthia, I haven't come across an impossible situation yet. There *is* hope for you."

"How? How?"

"First, there's a rulebook to live by. If you obey the rules it gives, I guarantee you'll have peace of mind. And it's one of the most exciting books you'll ever read!"

"A rulebook?"

"Yes, and I think you've heard of it. We call it the Holy Bible."

"Yeah, I went to Sunday school with the neighbor girl once or twice when I was little. I remember the teacher had a Bible. She said it helps people to read the Bible. Maybe that's what I need to do?"

"I'll tell you what, Cynthia. Let's walk back to the counseling center. I want to show you from the Bible how you can be a completely different person. Within the next half hour, your world can make a complete about-face!"

"Marji, I really don't know you. I've just heard people tell about you and your work. I was so desperate that I was ready to try anything. Now I can see why the people talk about you down here. You're different. I feel I can trust you."

Back at the counseling center, we sat together on the sofa. I opened my Bible and began to show Cynthia how to find the peace she so desperately wanted.

As I opened my Bible, I thought about when I had first come down here to the Lower East Side. I was so worried about how I was going to tell people how to be saved. But when I started doing it, the Holy Spirit helped me and made up for whatever I lacked.

My Bible now almost automatically fell open to the Book of Romans, the sixth book in the New Testament. I pointed to chapter three, verse twenty-three, and had Cynthia read it aloud with me: "For all have sinned, and come short of the glory of God."

I pointed out that the Bible says that all people are sinners and are unable to save themselves. They need someone else to save them. "God provided that Someone in Jesus." I told her, and we read together from the Gospel of John, chapter three, verse sixteen:

"For God so loved the world, that he gave his only begotten Son, that whosoever believeth in him should not perish, but have everlasting life."

I recounted the beautiful story of how Jesus, the pure and sinless Son of God, had left heaven to live in the filth of this earth and to die on the cross—not for His sins, but for ours.

The message was getting through.

"Now, Cynthia, listen to this," I said as I turned to the Book of First John, near the back of the New Testament. "I want you to see chapter one, verse nine. This is what it says: 'If we confess our sins, he is faithful and just to forgive us our sins, and to cleanse us from all unrighteousness.' "

I told her, "God will always keep His word. That's something you can always count on. Now look at that verse again. If you confess your sins to Him, what has He guaranteed that He will do?"

She read it haltingly: "To forgive . . . ."

"That's right! What else?"

"And to cleanse us from all unrighteousness."

"From how much of your unrighteousness has He promised to cleanse you?" I pointed to the word *all*.

She read it: "All!"

I could tell the light was dawning. The Holy Spirit was doing His work.

"Is that all there is to it?" she asked.

"That's where it starts, Cynthia. Wouldn't you like to pray to Jesus now?"

"Oh, yes! Yes! I need Jesus!"

Then very simply she prayed the sinner's prayer, asking Jesus to come into her heart and make her into a new person in Him. She was born again!

Talk about an immediate change in somebody! She was so happy, so overflowing with joy. She cried and she laughed and she cried some more. "I feel so clean, so new, so free!" she told me over and over again.

Then I told her about the Walter Hoving Home. She decided this was what she needed now, so I called and made arrangements for her to go there. I knew she was going to have the shock of her life when she got there. It was so clean and warm and inviting there. Such a contrast to her dingy apartment, where I had walked with her to get her few things together.

This time I also remembered to call Aunt Amilda, so she wouldn't worry about me.

Patsy was waiting for me at the home. She looked so good, so happy, so healthy. And I could see that, through the program, she was growing in the Lord.

That evening, back at the apartment, I shared with Aunt Amilda and Uncle Alex about Cynthia and told them how Patsy was getting along. They were as excited as I was. One more person had been born into God's kingdom!

After that, more and more girls started coming to me for help. They had heard about Patsy and Cynthia. And I still spent some time on the streets at night, telling girls about how Jesus could help them. Uncle Alex and Aunt Amilda always went with me. They could talk to some of the older people, while I spent time with the young girls. A lot of the prostitutes were in their early teens!

Well, the weeks turned into months, and the months into years. I was so satisfied with the ministry God had given me. Of course, there were still unanswered questions.

Every once in a while, I would meet a fine Christian young man. I'm very human, and I wondered if I would ever get married. If I did, would the Lord expect me to stay here and work? Would my future husband feel as I do about these people? I knew that could be a real problem. And yet I still felt such a deep desire to get married and share my life with someone else. Was this desire from God? Maybe I should pray harder for a husband. But maybe it was best for me to stay single.

Another problem was that Luigi Columbo was still around. As more people came to my counseling center, his business got worse. Every so often I would see him. He would clench his fist and scowl. I knew he was still trying to think of a way to get rid of me. But I had a lot of friends now, and he had to be careful.

And Benny Barnes was still around. He hadn't been arrested yet. Every time I talked to one of his girls, I knew I was opening her and me to problems.

Stephany was one of his girls; she was the third girl I took up to the Walter Hoving Home. Well, the following night Benny came up behind me on the street and stuck his switchblade at my ribs. There were a lot of people around, so he didn't dare stab me then. But he whispered, "Preacher lady, one of these nights you're going to wake up with my switchblade buried in your heart!"

Maybe so, but God had taken care of me so far.

And I was still concerned about Mom and Dad. They hadn't yet yielded their lives to Christ, as I had hoped they would. But I was still praying for them and believing it would happen.

Dad came down to the counseling center every once in a while. He still wanted me to give up my work on the Lower East Side and join his company. He even intimated he'd find a place for Uncle Alex in the business if I would go into the executive program he had outlined for me. I don't think he was trying to bribe me. I think he knew my life was still in danger, and that really worried him.

Well, things were going so well that my counseling center was becoming too small, and I just couldn't leave. Some nights we would hold Bible studies at the center, and the place was absolutely packed out. People were squeezed into every available space!

I wondered if I should try to find a bigger place. Yet I was praying that Luigi Columbo would have to close his porno shop because of the positive influence of God's place. So I really didn't want to move yet. If I moved, it would be a triumph of sorts for Luigi. But we were going to have to have more room.

The drug problem in the area worsened. I was able to help a few girls, but I knew it was a drop in the bucket compared to the need. So many people were in utter despair.

What could one poor little rich girl do? Not very much, obviously. But God had already helped me do more than anyone, including myself, had thought possible. So somehow I knew I had to stay for now. Somehow God was going to work out these problems. Whether it was a husband for me, my folks' salvation, the dangers from Luigi and Benny, or whoever and whatever, God had to answer prayer.

I was staking my life on that!

Some good things are happening at The Walter Hoving Home.

Dramatic and beautiful changes have been taking place in the lives of many girls since the Home began in 1967. Ninety-four percent of the graduates who have come with problems such as narcotic addiction, alcoholism and delinquency have found release and happiness in a new way of living—with Christ. The continued success of this work is made possible through contributions from individuals who are concerned about helping a girl gain freedom from enslaving habits. Will you join with us in this work by sending a check?

The Walter Hoving Home
Box 194
Garrison, New York 10524
(914) 424-3674

Your Gifts Are Tax Deductible

The Walter Hoving Home.

and blew in her face. She pulled back, laughing. They lay for a moment in silence, in the easy stillness of a new kind of intimacy.

"How did you meet Henry?" Callahan said finally.

"Staring at a Rothko."

He turned and gave her a deadpan look. "What's that? Some kind of dishwasher?"

"The painter."

"Ah."

"As though you didn't know. I worked in a gallery. And one day Henry came in."

"How old were you?"

"Way too young."

"But you stayed together."

"It was over long ago. We both know that." She hesitated. "We stayed together for Jimmy."

"You love him very much, don't you?"

Sarah nodded, and for a moment her smile was faraway, in another place. "The best and the brightest, my Jimmy," she said.

They kissed, then Callahan turned quickly away. He rose from the bed and began to dress. His expression was troubled. "You know, I need to start making plans to go to New York. I have to see Elliot's parents and tell them what happened."

"How long will you be away?"

"I don't know," he said, avoiding her eyes. "No idea . . ."

She reached out and touched his arm. "Nick—

what is this? One minute you're so loving and then this coldness, this distance. What are you doing? I don't understand. . . ."

He turned on her suddenly, his voice constricted with emotion. "I'm absolutely crazy about you, Sarah. I can't stop thinking about you. You're always in my mind, you're in my heart, you're in every fucking beat of me. But I can't go there with you. I can't do it. Look what happens to people around me. I'm not good for you."

"That's not true!"

"No, listen to me. Believe me, if I could live this life again I'd never leave you for a second. But you belong with your family and I belong here, and there's nothing I can do about it, because whichever way I look at it, somebody always gets hurt."

He hung in the doorway about to leave, when he suddenly lunged forward for one last passionate kiss.

"Sarah . . ."

And then he was gone. Sarah stared at the doorway, now empty of the man she loved. Tears filled her eyes.

PART
3

Excited preparations were underway for Sarah's thirty-third birthday. "Christ's year," she told her friends with a wry grin. "The dangerous one."

Jimmy, now ten and a handsome miniature version of his father, was lighting the last of thirty-three candles on a birthday cake. It took him five matches and a scorched finger but he was in high good spirits. Henry hovered over him, smiling. Jimmy lit the last candle and blew out the match.

"Ready, son?" Henry said.

"Ready." With boyish care, his shoulders hunched up in concentration, Jimmy carried the glowing cake into the living room. Lawrence and Lillias Bauford sat near the piano where their granddaughter Anna, a pretty young girl of five, sat playing a soft etude. She was an extremely gifted musician, considered a prodigy by the best tutors London could offer. Where Jimmy was the carbon copy of his father, Anna did not resemble him at all. In fact, except for her small, up-tilting nose and high forehead, she looked very little like Sarah.

Characteristically, though, Charlotte cut right to the point the first time she laid eyes on baby Anna. "That little jaw," she said. "Those eyes. So determined. And those jug ears. Where did *they* come from?" She studied her sister. "You know who I see in her features?"

"I know who you see," Sarah said, and at that moment she made a momentous decision. She would not go through life holding the secret to herself, sharing it with no one.

She told Charlotte that six weeks after returning from Cambodia she learned that she was pregnant with Nick Callahan's child. She had waited for Nick to call her, to arrange to come for her, but the weeks had passed—the weeks turned into months—until she finally accepted that she wasn't going to hear from him. She had held off sleeping with Henry, planning to leave him to go to Nick, but the pregnancy forced her to make a desperate decision. She could go off with Jimmy, risk the censure of her family and Henry's, have the baby and raise two children as a single mother. But did she have the strength and resolve to do that? And was she so certain that she no longer loved Henry? He had made a clean breast of his short-lived affair with Beatrice and had sworn that never again, as long as he lived, would he be unfaithful to her. She had used Beatrice as an excuse not to sleep with Henry, but two days after she learned of her pregnancy, after a pleasant evening spent with his parents and the consumption of far too much vintage wine, she allowed him to seduce her. Exactly seven months later Anna was born—"Two months premature," she told Charlotte, and only she and her obstetrician knew the truth. Anna weighed five pounds at birth—light but not suspiciously so—and no one voiced concerns or asked pointed questions, although Sarah sometimes felt uneasy around her mother-in-law. Lillias Bauford was a shrewd, worldly woman, and nothing, especially something of a scandalous nature, escaped her notice. Once, when Anna threw a temper tantrum—Jimmy had stolen a cookie from her plate—Mrs. Bauford looked at Sarah searchingly, with the hint of a smile, and said, "Henry is so terribly even tempered—and so are you, Sarah. Where do these volcanic eruptions come from, do you suppose?" It was as though Lillias had somehow divined the truth, and there always seemed to be a restraint between the child and her grandmother, a curious hint of formality. But Lawrence Bauford made up for it by loving the pretty, gifted girl unconditionally, lavishing presents on her at every opportunity.

The living room that Jimmy entered proudly with his mother's flaming cake was in dramatic contrast to their humble apartment of five years ago. Henry had managed to make it all the way back. Shortly before Anna was born he rejoined his father and extended the business into the burgeoning field of IPOs, concentrating on high-tech start-up companies; he was now in charge of the most profitable division of Bauford Investment Banking. His success and the excitement of Anna's impending birth had eased the tensions between Henry and Sarah, and there was enough residual affection between them to keep the marriage going. Still, Henry sometimes was haunted by the feeling that he had lost her, that he no longer inhabited her soul. She often seemed to be so far away—lost to him. He blamed the distance between them on his shocking lack of control with Beatrice all those years ago when he'd been at his lowest point. It never occurred to him that Sarah could have fallen out of love with him for any reason independent of Beatrice. In the beginning of their relationship he had often agonized as to why she had chosen him in the first place when there were so many more worthy suitors. But once they were married he could not conceive that she would change. In Henry's upper-class heart and soul, once you got married you stayed married. Maybe an occasional dalliance, yes, that was possible, especially for a man, but not anything serious enough to jeopardize a marriage.

Sarah applauded along with the others as Jimmy placed the cake carefully on the table. She was dressed in an expensive pants suit, designed by a fashionable London couturier, and Louis Vuitton shoes. Since his newfound success Henry had become obsessed with buying clothes and gifts for Sarah. He felt that his generosity was based on love; Sarah saw it as guilt.

Henry nodded at Anna, who began to bang out a rousing rendition of "Happy Birthday," and everyone joined in. After another round of applause, Sarah rose and kissed her children.

"Thank you, Anna. Thank you, Jim. That was lovely playing and a lovely cake."

"My playing was lovelier than his cake," Anna exploded, her hazel eyes blazing.

Jimmy, more easygoing, grinned and said, "Sure, Anna, but remember one thing. Nobody can eat your notes."

Sarah said quickly and firmly, "They are exactly as lovely as each other."

"Quite right," Lillias Bauford put in, with a glance at her granddaughter. "Let's not forget. This party is in honor of your mother."

Anna looked away and made a disgusted face at her brother, who stuck out his tongue. Not to be outdone, she stuck out her tongue and made a farting sound with her lips.

"Enough," Sarah said sharply. "Both of you."

"I'd cut the cake if I were you," Henry said. "So many candles on it. It might catch fire."

Sarah wagged a finger at him and grinned. "Really, dear. I'm not *that* old."

"Wait till they put one candle on for every decade," Mrs. Bauford said. "Then you'll know the meaning of ancient."

Her husband burst into laughter. "Quite right, old dear."

As Sarah leaned in to blow out the candles, Anna called out, *"Don't forget to make a wish, Mom. . . ."*

Sarah paused, grinning at her daughter's feistiness. The thought crossed her mind as it so often did. . . . *if he could see her . . . if only he could see her just once . . .* She took a deep breath, shut her eyes and blew. More cheers and applause.

And this is my wish. That he could see Anna, know her, see himself in her eyes, in her fiery temperament, in her brilliance . . .

After cake and ice cream, Anna sat on Grandpa Bauford's knee. He was slightly drunk from numerous glasses of sherry and wheezing heavily. He had had two heart attacks in the past year and suffered from emphysema. He adored Anna and it was obvious that he was partial to her, countering Lillias's clear preference for Jimmy. He stroked her dark hair, and, playing the old soak, a role she adored, he said, "Girl's a bloody prodigy. Plays like Steinway. No—hang on—they make 'em. Damn. Who was that chap . . . white hair . . . tickled the ivories."

"Rubenstein?" Sarah said.

"Yes, a stein—*Bern*stein. That's the chap."

"No more sherry for you," Mrs. Bauford said.

"Grandpa's funny," Anna said, giggling.

She slipped off his knee and hopped away to play.

"Ignore him," Mrs. Bauford said to her, a touch stiffly. "He's being silly."

But the girl ignored her as she spun a top on the hallway floor.

Henry sat next to his father, puffing on a cigar. "Did I tell you, Dad? Sarah's delivering her acceptance speech tomorrow at the UN luncheon."

"Oh, eh? Did a lousy job in Cyprus. Bunch of wankers." Catching his wife's warning glance, he added, "They're harmless, of course."

Sarah smiled, untroubled by her father-in-law's comments. As he had grown older and frailer, he increasingly enjoyed playing the clown. She had come to appreciate him through the years. Unlike his wife and son, he genuinely cared about the have-nots of the world; in his quiet, club man's way he had done much good and she respected him for that. Now, at the end of his life, he was an old silver-backed gorilla, and she felt he should be able to enjoy his damn sherry and all else be damned!

"I hope we're better than just harmless, Dad," she said.

"Tough business," he mumbled. "A watchman without a gun." He held out his glass. "A touch of sherry, Henry."

Henry glanced at his mother, who shrugged.

"Just don't moan and complain tonight, dear," she said. "I don't want to hear it."

When the party ended and the children were tucked in for the night, Henry held Sarah and kissed her cheek. "Happy birthday," he whispered softly in her ear.

"Thank you."

"Has it been a good one for you?"

"Yes."

"I want you to be happy, Sarah."

"I know you do."

He handed her a small, gift-wrapped box. "For you."

She slowly undid the wrapping, careful not to tear the silver paper, and pulled out an emerald necklace.

"Henry—this must have cost a fortune. You don't need to be so extravagant."

"Nothing's too good for you."

"Really!" She made a wry face.

"Christmas bonus," he said. "The new genetics company is soaring, the stock's going through the roof." He looked at her anxiously. "Do you really like them?"

"I do." She kissed his cheek. "Thank you. You're a very generous man, very giving."

He took the necklace from her and started to put it around her neck. But she pulled back, tensing up. "They wouldn't look right with this dress," she said. She yawned, not bothering to cover her mouth. "I'm beat. It's been a long day. Will you be staying up long?"

"Not long," he said.

"Good night, then."

He watched her climb the stairs, a smile of disappointment pinching his face.

The day that Sarah had been looking forward to for so long had finally arrived. She was to be officially installed as UNHCR's chief officer in the United Kingdom. It was a great honor and she knew that she was deserving of it; she had worked long and hard, with both passion and great competence. The night before the luncheon meeting she stayed up until the early hours of the morning fine-tuning her speech for perhaps the tenth time. She wanted it to be exactly right, to hit on all the salient points of charitable work and to walk the fine line between seriousness and the light touch.

By noon the hotel ballroom was filled to capacity. Sarah sat at the speaker's table staring out at the assemblage of politicians, diplomats, lobbyists, and the press, most of whom she knew. She smiled as the flashbulbs went off and listened attentively to Michael Braithwaite, a wealthy donor and a social force in the city.

He said, "Many of you know Sarah from her work with the Elliot Hauser Foundation on International Promotion of Human Rights. In more recent years she has become an active lobbyist in Whitehall on issues of asylum and refugee protection. Ladies and Gentlemen, it gives me great pleasure to introduce our new spokesperson for the UNHCR in the United Kingdom—Mrs. Sarah Bauford."

There was an enthusiastic round of applause. Sarah stepped up to the microphone, spread her notes out on the dais and turned to the speaker.

"Thank you, Michael, for those kind words." She added with a smile, "Certainly more than I deserve." She stared out at the audience, touching her notes nervously. "Ladies and Gentlemen, I feel somewhat awed—or perhaps thunderstruck, a favorite word of my mother's—standing here in front of you. But I am also honored, in particular, because UNHCR was the organization to which I was first introduced by my friend and mentor, Elliot Hauser."

Sarah cleared her throat, hesitated, and took a sip of water as she watched Charlotte rush into the room, trench coat billowing behind her. She hurried over to Henry's table, greeted him with a quick kiss and slid into a seat beside him.

Sarah continued, saying, "I know that my being offered this position would have given Elliot enormous pleasure, and I wish more than anything that I could tell him how proud I am to accept." She shot a quick glance at Charlotte, who nodded encouragingly. She knew how much her little sister hated public speaking.

"Elliot Hauser taught me many things," she continued. "He taught me that we can make a difference, however small. As he used to say, 'The only thing evil needs to triumph is for good people to stand by and do nothing.'"

For a moment an image of Elliot flashed through her mind. He lay dead on the ground in Cambodia in a pool of his own blood. She forced the image away, one that had inhabited so many of her dreams.

She leaned against the podium and said, "Over fifty million people—think about it, fifty million!—are refugees or displaced persons in the world today, and because of closed minds and funding shortfalls, we're only able to reach half of those in need."

She hesitated momentarily, faltering over the last phrase. When she picked up the water glass her hand was trembling. Henry and Charlotte watched her with concern. They sensed that something was wrong.

She bent over her notes and said finally, "So we rely on our partners—the network of aid groups blazing a trail across crises as they arise, in El Salvador, Angola, Chechnya, Sri Lanka. Those NGOs—the brave nongovernmental groups—from Oxfam right down to the smallest outfits . . . run . . . run by people like Elliot Hauser . . ."

Suddenly she saw Nick Callahan in the sea of expectant faces. He was staring at her, waiting for her to continue. He was there, he was smiling—then he was gone in a flash. She fumbled with her notes. She had lost her train of thought, her place in the progression of the speech. She jumped ahead and said haltingly, ". . . and I pray for those who survive him, who continue his work . . . without security or certainty . . . wherever they may be in the world. . . ."

She shook her head, too upset to continue. She mumbled, "Thank you," gathered up her notes and hurried offstage. The crowd buzzed. Henry turned to Charlotte. "What on earth happened?"

"I'll go to her, Henry. Take her out for"—she grinned—"well, not for tea and sympathy exactly. More like strong coffee and a sister-to-sister chat."

Half an hour later Charlotte and Sarah sat in Holland Park, on the very bench where Sarah had had a rainy reunion with Elliot so many years ago, on that day when she had made the fateful decision to return to the field and to all that followed from it—Elliot's death, the realization of her love for Nick Callahan and the conception of Anna in their one brief coupling. She had been so impossibly young and naïve back then. It seemed impossible that she was the same person. It seemed to her that a lifetime had passed between then and now, and yet that past swept over her in pounding waves of memory.

The sisters sat in companionable silence. Charlotte studied the gray sky.

"Quite a climate you have," she said. "I'm surprised the suicide rate isn't higher here."

"I guess the British are too reserved to call attention to themselves."

"Well, there's a theory."

Sarah took Charlotte's hand and gripped it tight. "Thanks for coming"—she grinned ruefully—"to Sarah's disaster."

"Hey, I fly thousands of miles to see my baby sister give a speech. I have a backache and jet lag. What's a taxi ride to the park with a crazy girl? No big deal."

"I'm sorry. I really blew it, didn't I? I'll bet everybody's furious. I wouldn't blame them."

"Who cares? Fuck 'em."

"That's easy for you to say."

"You want the truth? I think they actually enjoyed your emotional pratfall. 'She's nuts' is an exciting change from 'wonderful speech.' Who doesn't love a car wreck?"

Sarah nodded, gathering her thoughts.

"Something on your mind, li'l sis? Let's have it. Mother Freud is growing impatient."

"I got a letter from Nick," she said. "Five years and he's never written."

"Typical male scoundrel. Leaves his calling card and then absconds with your heart."

"He knows about Anna. I finally had to write him."

"Did he mention Anna in his letter?"

"No."

"I would say that's a little thoughtless, even for Nick."

"I don't care about that, Charlie. I think he's in trouble."

"What kind of trouble? Did he say anything?"

"No. Just how he was—little things. The usual medical foul-ups. But I don't think he's telling the truth—or he's holding something back."

"He's in Chechnya, isn't he? I heard about him when I was there, but had no way of getting in touch."

"He's running some sort of camp, but I don't know exactly. He was vague on the details." Sarah squeezed her sister's hand. "I have to find him. It's a feeling I have—that he needs me."

"You think your going would really help? You'd better give this some careful thought, sweetie. Chechnya is a rough, crime-ridden place. People disappear very suddenly and are never seen again.

There's a civil war going on, their Russian neighbors are trying to free the Muslim Caucasus from Soviet domination. A real mess—a cauldron of bloody ethnic violence. It's sort of like the Old West before there were any laws."

"I've followed your reports."

"And they're true. Every word is true."

Sarah sighed, but her expression was resolute. "You have contacts, Charlie. You're going back there, aren't you?"

"Too soon, I'm afraid. I have to keep up my reputation as Miss Intrepid Reporter."

"You can find out where he is and I'll join you there. I need to see him."

Charlotte regarded her sister seriously.

"I can see that this is one love that hasn't died."

"I need to see him," Sarah repeated. She had that steely look in her eyes—the look of total determination. Even as a child she could cow her clever sister with that look.

"I'm telling you Chechnya is the pits. No place is worse."

"I don't care."

"Okay—I'll see what I can do."

"Honestly?"

"Do I have any choice?" Charlotte said with a smile.

"Nope."

"If I hear anything, or can wangle an interview, I'll call you."

"Thank you, Charlie. Love you."

"Love you, too, crazy girl."

They sat on the bench in silence, holding hands, each deep in her own thoughts.

This time when Sarah made her plans to leave London she did not share them with Henry. She still cared about her husband—he was a decent man, he was a good father—but she could not hide from the truth, as hard as she had tried. She no longer loved him, not the way you're supposed to love a husband, and she hadn't loved him that way for years, if she ever truly had. The moment she met Nick Callahan, her love for Henry had begun to die. She tried for years to make the best of a relationship that was increasingly rent with tension and unspoken misunderstandings. She had been brought up to believe that marriage was a serious commitment, not an extended date as it was for some of her friends. There were bound to be good times and bad times, and you were expected to appreciate the good times just as you soldiered through the bad ones. But once Anna was born it became harder for Sarah to rationalize the way she was living, the essential lie. Anna was Nick Callahan's child. If only Nick had called from the States after they had parted at Heathrow. If only she had had the chance to tell him she was carrying his child. But all of that was suddenly beside the point. He was in trouble and needed her. She had to go to him.

It took Charlotte three weeks to make arrangements for the sisters to meet in Chechnya. On the night Sarah was leaving Henry had arranged a dinner at his club for important clients from Munich. Her plan was to be gone by the time he returned home. She read Anna's favorite story to her that night, *Snow White*. She never tired of it.

Sarah read softly. " . . . And the prince climbed the stairs to the bedroom and carefully pushed open the door. There on the bed lay the beautiful Snow White. The prince knelt beside the bed and kissed her. . . ."

Anna yawned and crushed her fists to her eyes. She was almost asleep. "Maybe I'll have a prince someday, Mummy."

"I'm sure you will, darling."

"Boys—eew! They're so yucky. Do you think the prince is yucky?"

"No. Definitely not."

"You don't have to read anymore," Anna said through another huge yawn. "I'll miss you, Mummy."

"I'll only be gone a week—ten days at the most."

"Is ten days longer?"

"Yes."

Anna nodded. "I know that. A week is seven days long. I can name the days of the week, too."

"I know you can. And what day of the week were you born on?"

"A Sunday." Her eyes fluttered and closed. "Goodnight, Mummy."

"Goodnight, my darling. Pleasant dreams."

"Don't let the bedbugs bite," the girl mumbled and seconds later she was sound asleep.

Sarah checked her watch: ten o'clock. She tiptoed into Jimmy's room and gently kissed his forehead. He had soccer practice before school in the morning and had gone to sleep early. His skin felt warm and moist and he smelled of toothpaste. She removed one of his blankets. She hovered over him for a moment with tears in her eyes. "There are things I can't help," she whispered out loud. "I hope they don't hurt you too much, Jim, and that you'll learn to understand and forgive. I can't stand the thought of hurting you or giving you any pain. I love you too much."

She tiptoed down the stairs and slipped quietly toward the front door. From her shoulder bag she removed an envelope with "Henry" scrawled across the front. She placed it on a side table near the door. As she was putting on her coat, she gave a little gasp of surprise and fear. Henry was standing in the shadows of the staircase staring at her.

"Henry? I thought you were at the club. You're home early."

He switched on a light. His eyes were glazed with pain, his smile was tight and unconvincing, and he kept clasping and unclasping his hands.

"Do you really think you can just walk away?"

She let the shoulder bag slip down to her feet. "I'm sorry."

He reached for the banister for support. She knew he had been drinking, probably far too much; he did that with important clients. "So this is it, is it? Ten years up in smoke."

"Please Henry . . ."

"Up in fucking smoke."

"You're going to wake the children."

"The children . . . Yes. You kiss the children good-bye. You scribble a quick note, then you sneak off into the night."

"I'm not leaving the children," she said. "I love them more than anything. You know that."

"But you are leaving me." Tears gathered in his eyes; he made no attempt to wipe them away.

"This is so hard," she said. "Nothing I say is going to help."

"You could've told me. We could've talked this through. Sought help. But this—I mean writing a *note?*"

"I thought it would be the easiest way. We have talked, you know. Talked and talked. But what good has it done us? It's just the same old conversation. Nothing is solved. The hurt just goes deeper."

"I don't want a divorce," he said. "I don't want that." He shook his head, gripping the banister more tightly, and Sarah could see that he was more desperate than angry. A wave of compassion rose within her, but she held it in check.

They stood in silence until Sarah said, "Please tell the kids I won't be gone long. We'll talk about it when I come back."

Henry sought her gaze, his expression softening until at last he conceded the truth with a nod. His gentle eyes filled with tears, and Sarah felt her own eyes began to smart. But she knew that she couldn't linger. It would be even harder for both of them if she did. Besides, there were no words; there was no manual providing neat, clean instructions on how to end a marriage.

She took a deep breath and turned to step across the threshold. An instant later, she disappeared into the night.

S arah wore a heavy coat on top of two thick sweaters and still she was cold. The Land Rover had a defective heater that gave only a whisper of warmth. The driver skillfully maneuvered along the potted road. He spoke passable English (he was a Danish volunteer), but he was taciturn by nature. Sarah would start a conversation and then after one or two brief exchanges they would lapse into silence.

It was hard to believe that only twenty-four hours earlier she had worn a light topcoat in London's moist and mild autumn and now the world was white and barren and the wind sliced through her and her bones ached. Snow swirled over the jagged Caucasus mountains and the terrain in the distance was empty, as though they were approaching the very end of the earth.

They churned through the icy sludge and passed a number of strange shaped Russian military vehicles half frozen in the snow and abandoned. As they approached Grozny the landscape became littered with crude, stone buildings with broken windows; some of them even lacked doors. The buildings looked uninhabitable and yet people occasionally entered and emerged from them. A few trudging locals buried in overcoats scuttled here and there under the watchful eyes of Russian soldiers.

As the Land Rover rolled into the war-gutted city, Sarah had her face pressed to the icy window, awed by the scale of destruction. The intense silence of the countryside they had driven through was now shattered by the sounds of traffic, blasting horns, and the loud symphony of Russian and Chechen dialects. She watched as a woman hauling shopping bags took off across the street, glancing fearfully over her shoulder as she went. The driver braked cautiously on the slippery road to avoid hitting her. Suddenly a pack of civilians raced up the street, away from the Land Rover, in collective terror. They were fleeing sniper fire. An older woman carrying a small child fell to the ground, shot in the leg. She waved the child on. The boy raced away, leaving the old lady in a writhing heap.

Sarah, her face pressed to the window, stared at

the woman, then turned to the driver. "What can we do?"

"Nothing," he answered. "This is a daily occurrence."

"Will someone help her?"

"Probably not. You're in Grozny. No one can afford to help anyone else."

She turned to look at the young Danish volunteer, so bitter and withdrawn. He must have been, at least at the beginning, idealistic enough to offer his services to this war-ravaged part of the world, but the face he revealed to her was hard, unconcerned. He began speaking into the radio in Chechen. "Snipers. Karolky Street. I'm getting out of here. I'll take the XYZ bypass."

"What did you say?" Sarah asked him.

He repeated his words in English as he leaned forward and stared intently through the windshield. Ten minutes later he pulled up at the Grozny Hotel. He hopped out and handed Sarah her bags.

"Good luck," he said solemnly.

"Thank you."

"You're going to need it." He turned away before she could answer and drove off.

Sarah entered the hotel and was given directions to the pressroom, which was a five-minute walk toward the center of the city. Charlotte greeted her at the door and they embraced for a moment, overcome with emotion.

"Welcome to hell," Charlotte said finally. She managed a grin. "At least this fucking room is heated. They say that Grozny offers you two choices. You can either get shot or freeze to death." She took Sarah's arm. "Come on. I've got some footage you'll want to see."

The pressroom was packed with reporters and photographers. The noise level was deafening and a blue haze of cigarette smoke hung over the room, which, Charlotte explained, was an abandoned factory space, converted into a press center. Journalists sat typing at laptops and talking on SAT phones. The crudely rigged lights in the room flickered on and off from the frequent explosions in the distance.

Charlotte hovered over Sarah, protective and edgy.

"Okay," Sarah said. "Let's run it."

Charlotte pressed "play," and a flickering image appeared on the monitor of a makeshift hospital crammed with tents and relief supplies in the shell of an old railroad siding. A sparse number of local medics were attending to the refugees as Russian soldiers patrolled the perimeter.

Callahan suddenly moved across the frame, speaking to the video camera which followed him.

"He looks older," Sarah said, frowning at the screen.

"Older and discouraged," Charlotte said. "But listen to him. The fire's still there."

He glared into the eye of the camera. " . . . And not a single Western leader has had a thing to say about what's going on here. No threats, no criticism, no fucking comment. Nothing. This place might as well not exist. And now we're all they have—a handful of doctors and volunteers—and they want us to save face for them. Well, *fuck* that. They should stop fucking about and get their arses out here." He shook his head, clearly annoyed at himself, and speaking straight into the camera he said, "Shit! All I'm doing is swearing. . . ."

"Don't worry," said a voice that Sarah recognized as Charlotte's. "Just let it come. We can edit it later."

"Okay," Callahan replied. "But just the swearing part. Leave all the rest in."

"Right, Nick. Just keep going. The camera's on."

"Well—basically—what I'm saying is, nothing's changed. Not from where I'm standing. I've done Ethiopia, Pakistan, Cambodia, Somalia, and Bosnia—the same old shit wherever you go—and it's going to go on until we stop pretending our loyalty ends with the arseholes on our stamps. I mean, fuck sovereignty. I'm talking about basic human rights, you know? One body, one soul. The same for every fucking one of us. The right of every mother and child to—"

The rest was lost in a crack of gunfire; the

video frame whipped around, wildly projecting odd angles. The scene was chaotic: Callahan running, hands raised to protect his face; a Russian soldier screaming as he swung his rifle around in wide arcs; a grenade sailing through the air as the camera swooped in to catch it in flight; an explosion followed by a number of Russian soldiers dead, wounded, moaning; Callahan now struggling with two men in ski masks; breaking away and running again; a blur of images as the camera smashed to the ground, followed by blackness, nothing.

"Jesus," Sarah breathed.

"You okay?"

Sarah still stared at the blank screen. "Nick . . ."

"We don't know where he is. Nobody's contacted us yet. We think bandits are behind it—Chechens—after money. And in a way that's good. They may come after us for ransom. If it was purely political they'd have shot him on the spot."

"I know he's still alive, Charlie. I just know it." She squeezed her sister's arm. "You took a terrible risk."

"A perk of the job," Charlotte said. "I hope you're right about Nick. All we can do is wait and keep the faith."

A big bear of a man walked up to them and gave Charlotte a peck on the cheek. He wore a soiled flak jacket and a thick scarf wound loosely around his neck.

"Sarah, this is Bob Strauss. He's with the ICRC here. He's been helping us."

Sarah and Strauss shook hands. His smile was warm and Sarah was immediately drawn to him.

"She's concerned about Nick," Charlotte said. "I ran the tape for her."

He nodded, and his heavy features drew together in a frown. "Well, the net result right now is, we don't know who took him. We're not sure if he pissed off the Russians or the Chechens. We're pretty sure there's a motive." His expression changed to a sad smile as he added, "You know Nick. He could piss off the Pope."

"What was he doing here?"

Strauss hesitated and shot a quick look at Charlotte. "I guess you know he isn't just a doctor anymore."

Sarah tried to read his eyes. "No, I didn't know."

"He's a coordinator—an administrator, I guess you could say. He's working on a new water system for the city. He's very popular, you know, but he rubs authorities the wrong way. He doesn't like playing games with a corrupt system. Compromise isn't in his playbook."

"So how do we find him?"

"Well . . ." He glanced again at Charlotte, who said nothing, then back at Sarah. "Nobody I've spoken to has any leads—not yet anyway. If he's in the hands of the Mafia the only thing we can do is wait. They're bound to make some sort of demand eventually. Nick is pretty well known."

Sarah shook her head impatiently. "Can't we offer a reward? I don't see why we have to sit and wait. There must be *something* we can do."

Strauss listened to her calmly. He said, "The best thing for you to do, ma'am, is stay in the hotel for a couple of days. Be patient. We'll see what turns up."

Charlotte and Sarah walked back to the hotel through the war-torn city. They walked fast and tried to ignore the intermittent thunder of gunfire in the distance. Sarah was completely focused, eyes front, and Charlotte had to trot to stay up with her. She was concerned about her sister. She knew that Sarah was capable of taking tremendous risks in a crisis. Charlotte remembered the time when Sarah was a teenager—too young for a driver's license—and she had received a call from a school friend who had overdosed on acid and had been raped. The girl had called her from a motel room eighty miles from San Francisco. Sarah had taken her father's car and had driven to her friend. "I drove a hundred all the way," she told Charlotte later. "I had to get to her."

That was Sarah. She would always do what had to be done, with little regard for obstacles.

"Look—I think Bob's right," Charlotte said. "You have to let this play itself out."

Sarah shook her head. "I didn't come all this way to twiddle my thumbs in a hotel room."

"Sarah—sweetie—listen to me. This is a very dangerous place."

"I've been in dangerous places before."

"Not like this. They'll take journalists, aid workers, anybody. There are no rules here. Don't for one second assume that you're immune."

"I'm not giving up now."

"You heard what Bob said—"

"He says that to everybody. His little mantra. Pacify the little lady. He seems like a nice guy, Charlie, but I know what he thinks."

Charlotte rested an arm on her sister's jacket. "Please think this out carefully," she said. "I love you, I want you safe. The thing you should do is go home, go back to London. There's nothing you can do here. I'll call you the minute I hear anything."

Sarah stopped walking and turned to her. "Go on, say it, Charlie. Say what's on your mind. I hate it when you pussyfoot around things."

Charlotte stared at her for a long moment. "When people disappear here," she said, "they don't come back."

The sisters regarded each other in silence. Sarah slowly shook her head, her lower lip pushed out. It was the old obstinacy, Charlotte realized.

Sarah could not be controlled when she reached this level of commitment to a goal. She had crossed a line and would do whatever she felt had to be done.

"I can't accept that," she said.

"It's the truth."

Slowly Sarah reached for her sister's hand. "Okay, I've been warned. I understand and you know how much I appreciate your concern. But you're not responsible for my actions."

"I know that."

"We're grown-up people now, Charlie."

"I know that, too."

"I can't let this go until I find him. Dead or alive."

She pulled Charlotte close and embraced her, their cheeks touching. "I love you," she said.

"I love you, li'l sis."

"Go to work now," Sarah said, smiling. "If you need me I'll be in the hotel."

With that, she turned and walked away, leaving Charlotte to watch her disappear around a corner. Charlotte raised a gloved hand and wiped tears from her eyes.

Sarah sat alone on a sagging bed in her hotel room sipping a glass of lukewarm tea, still wearing her coat to fight off the bitter cold. She was writing a letter to Jimmy and Anna when there was a knock at the door. She looked up, puzzled.

"Who is it?" she said. "Charlie, is that you?"

There was no answer. She got up stiffly—the cold seemed to have crept into her bones—and walked to the door.

"Who is it?"

There was still no answer. She thought of soldiers, the secret police, the Chechen Mafia. If it wasn't Charlotte it couldn't be good. Curiosity finally overcame her fear and she unbolted the door. Jan Steiger stood in the doorway, looking somewhat shriveled inside a too-large coat as though he had recently suffered a serious illness. His smile was faintly insinuating, she thought, and hinting at evil intent.

"Mrs. Bauford," he said. "I'm Jan Steiger, a friend of Nick Callahan's."

Sarah didn't move away from the entrance, but stood where she was, waiting for him to continue. She knew who Steiger was, and she also knew that he and Nick were not friends.

"May I come in?"

After a pause, she opened the door wider and moved to one side. Steiger stepped in, strolled to the window, glanced out, and then turned away. Her eyes followed his every move.

Steiger said, "We've worked together off and on. You should move your bed, by the way. It's too near the window."

"Has he been working for you?"

"Yes." He waved his hand back and forth in a

qualifying gesture. "In a manner of speaking."

After a tense pause Sarah said, "I'm sorry. Who told you I was here? Was it my sister, Charlotte Jordan? I know nobody in Grozny."

"Oh no," he replied. "I'm not a journalist, Mrs. Bauford. I'm more—well, I suppose you could say import-export." He smiled, although not, she noticed, with his small dark eyes. "You and I nearly met in Cambodia."

Sarah continued to stare at him. "I know who you are. But I still don't understand how you found me."

"It's unimportant. I have my sources."

"I'm sure you do, Mr. Steiger. Now what is it you want? I'm rather busy."

"Actually Nick mentioned you a few times." He did a brief but pointed survey of her face and legs and added, "I certainly can't blame him."

"What do you want?" Sarah repeated.

"I think we have this backward. I think the proper question is, What do *you* want, Mrs. Bauford?"

"I'm here to find Nick Callahan."

Steiger nodded. "You know, for a pair of tits you've sure got brass balls."

Sarah did not join his smile. She simply stood very still, waiting him out. He had come with an agenda and she was not going to help him get to it.

He spoke quickly now, saying, "The last I heard

he was being held in the mountains. A rebel position about five, six miles northeast of here. The entire area's under heavy shelling from the Russians right now, but I managed to make radio contact. They were negotiating. They know who he is."

Sarah let his words die in the room before she said, "Why are you telling me this?"

The look he gave her struck her for the first time as completely genuine. "I'm curious. I mean—you come out to this shithole-in-hell, you really think you're going to find him? What is this? Is this that thing called love? Is that what it is, Mrs. Bauford?"

Sarah did not answer, did not move. She waited.

"Okay," Steiger said with a shrug. "Whatever. You're here. Now here's the situation. If I get him back alive, I lose one less operative. On the other hand, if he's dead, he's dead. I'm not stupid enough to risk my own ass for some fucked-up big mouth. But you? You want to risk your life for . . . love?'" He chuckled softly, shaking his head in disbelief. "Jan Steiger will trade with anyone," he said. "Anyone at all."

Sarah let the silence stretch out and when she spoke her voice was absolutely level. "What do I do?"

"I have a friend, a local. He can get you to the mountains, but after that you're on your own." He smiled. "I'm just a spectator."

"That's the trade," she said. "I save you an operative."

"Correct, Mrs. Bauford. You save my operative. And you?" He laughed, a brief liquid bark. "You do it for love."

The pickup shot through a tunnel of trees weighted down with snow. In the far distance Sarah could see flashes of Russian artillery lighting the sullen sky. Steiger's driver—a Chechen mobster—wore American combat boots, dark glasses, and the macho stubble of a young rogue movie star. He drove with a kind of nonchalant audacity. Sarah, sitting beside him, kept her eyes trained on the rutted road ahead, her shoulder bag pressed to her lap. In the back of the pickup two bodyguards sat with their rifles angled out to both flanks.

The driver held his hand out. "Give me picture," he said.

Sarah handed him a Polaroid of Callahan and

her at the border in Thailand, happy and smiling. *We made love that day. Anna was created in that moment in the jungle, in the rain.*

The driver glanced quickly at it, then back to the road.

"Why you look for him?"

"I'm his wife," she said as she shot a glance at the driver's profile—cruel, handsome, although pitted with old acne scars.

He caught her eye. "Maybe he no come back. Then you find me, huh?" He grinned. "I show you big man."

Sarah returned his smile before quickly turning away to study the terrain ahead. The pickup was heading up into the mountains, and the landscape was vast, white, and barren. The going was slow now, the driver operating mainly in first gear. When they reached the outskirts of a rebel compound, two armed men approached the car.

"This as far as we go," the driver said, bringing the pickup to a sliding stop. "You pay me now."

"I paid Steiger."

He shrugged and grinned. "You pay me, too."

She handed him a wad of bills, which he stuck in his jacket without a glance. The rebels gestured to her to follow them, and they began to walk along a narrow mountain track, which ascended gradually. They walked in silence. The distant artillery seemed to be growing louder as Sarah followed the rebels along the icy path, occasionally sliding and stumbling, but she was determined to match their fast pace.

After about twenty minutes of strenuous hiking, chilled through her many layers of clothing, Sarah saw a small fire at a bend in the path where the ground leveled and widened and a makeshift perimeter had been established. Chechen rebels were moving about drinking and talking. Sarah approached the fire accompanied by one of the rebels. He spoke in Chechen to a bearded Muslim warlord, and the man nodded repeatedly, his expression impassive. The Muslim finally burst into a staccato monologue, all the time eyeing Sarah as she was being frisked for weapons.

"Do you speak any English?" she asked the Muslim.

He nodded gravely. "I do."

"I came to see Nick Callahan," she said. "The English doctor. United Nations."

She held out the photograph and he stared at it with a frown. He then grinned—a white circular break in his beard—and said something to his men in Chechen. He then extended his hand toward Sarah, rubbing his thumb and index finger together in the international signal for a money transfer. Sarah handed him a thick envelope.

"Please," Sarah said. "Do you know where he is? Have you seen him?"

Keeping his movements very casual, he glanced

once more at the photograph she had handed him, then dropped it in the fire. In seconds it curled into black nothingness. She watched the brief blaze without expression. She had prized that photograph; not a week had passed these past years when she hadn't looked at it and remembered. She sensed the violence in the air— it had a smell not unlike burning flesh.

"The troublemaker," the Muslim said. His eyes nearly closed as he squinted at her. "Come," he said finally.

He walked off, and a muscular rebel with a long mustache fell in close behind him, motioning for Sarah to follow them. They retraced their steps along the path leading to the camp until they came to a fork. They chose a narrow twisting track that descended into a forest of pine trees. As they walked on among the giant trees the path abruptly ended, but the Muslim warlord moved along with confident strides, sure of his direction. The boom of artillery was much closer now, mixed with the sound of machine-gun fire from helicopter gunships. The Muslim stopped and stared at the sky, moving his head back and forth, searching for something. He rubbed his hand over his beard in a series of nervous strokes. He spoke to the rebel in Chechen and his tone was urgent.

A few moments later they entered a small clearing, in the center of which stood a woodshed, buckled and leaning precipitously to one side in partial collapse. The second Sarah saw it she felt an ache in her chest; her heart pounded. The Muslim nodded toward the woodshed and said something to the rebel and they quickly disappeared into the trees.

Sarah began to run. "Nick!" she screamed.

She stumbled across the snow, lifted the beam that served as a lock and yanked it back. She stepped inside. The air inside was thick and fetid with human waste. She clicked on her flashlight and saw half-eaten food strewn on the floor and she saw several strands of severed nylon cords. At first glance the woodshed appeared to be empty, but then she heard the sound of faint breathing, like a sustained sigh, from a corner behind a pile of cut wood.

She moved closer. The beam of her flashlight picked out a ghostly face.

"Nick," she cried out, rushing to him.

The instant the flash hit him, he cowered back in terror. She squatted next to him and tentatively, tenderly touched his face.

"Nick. Nick? It's me—Sarah. . . ."

Slowly he opened his eyes and stared at her. He blinked as though trying to focus. His breathing was fast and harsh, his cheeks were caved in, his pallor deathly white. Trying to control her own panic at the sight of him, she stroked his hair. "Oh my love," she whispered. "What have they done to you?"

He was tied firmly to wide planks of wood that ran up his back and arms in a crucifixlike shape. He had a long, infected wound on his right thigh that was oozing pus. His forehead felt burning hot to her touch.

"Am I dead?" he said in a whisper.

"No, my darling, you're alive. You're here with me now. I've come to take you home."

He closed his eyes and slumped back against his crucifix.

"Nick?"

He shuddered and she could see his teeth chattering. "Cold . . . I'm so cold. . . ." He was shaking badly from the fever and hypothermia. Sarah covered him with her outer coat and pressed her body close to his. She talked to him, forcing his attention, fighting to keep him awake. She feared that if he slipped off he might not make it back to her.

There was a huge explosion, which Callahan barely registered. The artillery shells were honing in closer and closer to them now. Sarah began to work on the ropes that bound him to the planks and when he was free she had to pull him up; he was too weak to stand by himself.

"I'm very tired," he said.

"Those men who hurt you, they're gone. They're fighting the Russians. Can you hear them? Listen."

Gently she turned Callahan's head. He nodded slightly and a light appeared in his eyes.

"Nick, there's a Red Cross camp on the Inguisham—about four miles from here. We can walk there."

"No," he said faintly. "My leg."

"We have to. There's no choice."

He started to sink to the floor. It took all her strength to keep him on his feet.

Another shell landed, this one dangerously near, and the concussive sound made Sarah's ears ring.

"For God's sake, Nick," she shouted, "we have to get out of here. Come on—*you can do it.*"

She suddenly threw herself over Callahan, trying to shield him, as a fiery stream of gunfire rained down on the ceiling of the shack. The bombing was steady now.

"They're hitting the refugee camp," he said. "A few klicks east of here. I think they got the fuel dump."

He spoke without emotion, as though this was a scene in someone else's drama, not his own. She held him by the shoulders and stared straight into his eyes, willing him to listen.

"Do you remember what I wrote you?" She was speaking quickly, racing against time, time that was fast running out for both of them. "Do you remember I told you about Anna? Your daughter. You have a daughter, Nick."

"Anna . . ."

"That's right. And she's just like you. Black hair, burning hazel eyes, round and intense like yours.

And she's so full of opinions." Sarah was crying now. "You can't make her stop. She has opinions on everything under the sun." She pulled Callahan toward the door. "So come on, you can't give up now, you *can't*. She needs to know her daddy."

"Anna," he said. "My daughter. In Cambodia."

"One magical moment, Nick."

"I somehow knew even then. I had a feeling. . . ."

"But you never called."

"I couldn't." He shook his head despairingly.

He made the first feeble effort to move on his own. Sarah gripped him firmly, helping him to maintain his balance. Again he closed his eyes.

"Nick, goddamn it, stay awake. Talk to me. You hear that artillery? We have to move. *Come on* now."

"Four miles," he said. "I don't see how . . ." His voice trailed off.

A fiery burst erupted on the track only yards from the shed, spewing rocks and debris. Part of the wall collapsed and the entire structure shuddered on its foundation. The blast hurled Sarah and Callahan to the floor, and seconds later a tree, severed from its roots by the explosion, crashed across the entrance to the shed. A moment after that part of the roof caved in just missing them. They lay sprawled on the shed floor, snow falling on their upturned faces.

Slowly Sarah hauled herself to a sitting position; she had a hazy sense of surprise that she was still alive. Through the shattered shed entrance the tree-lined hills, crowned with white, stretched out to the horizon where the white dissolved into the gray of the sky. An eerie silence had descended; the bombardment was over.

She looked down at Nick. His eyes opened and he stared straight into hers with the hint of a smile. She sensed a renewed alertness in him, a touch of color in his cheeks, a greater clarity in his speech as he said, "That was close. I think I've used up most of my nine lives."

Sarah smiled and kissed him on the mouth, relieved that he finally seemed aware of his surroundings. She took a section of lining from the jacket she wore inside her heavy coat and made a tourniquet for Callahan's leg.

"It's pretty badly infected," she said.

"Sepsis," he muttered. "Not good."

They stepped out of the ravished woodshed, Callahan leaning on Sarah for support. "I'll get my sea legs in a minute," he said. "They had me bound pretty tight and the circulation's just coming back."

They saw smoke rising from the trees in the distance. "The rebel camp," he said. "I'm sure it's been destroyed." He kept looking behind him as though he expected to be jumped from the rear. "They'll be coming back, you know. We have to move."

He followed behind Sarah as they stumbled through hard-packed snow that crunched under their feet, fighting against a bitter wind flecked with ice that burned and tore at their exposed flesh. They walked for nearly an hour and Callahan grew steadily weaker. His leg finally gave out and he collapsed to his knees in the snow. Sarah hurried back to help him up. He studied their footprints with a frown as they disappeared into the distance. Sarah glanced at him anxiously.

"What is it?"

He pointed. "We're leaving a trail," he said. "I mean a lot of money to them. It won't be hard to track us."

"We have to keep walking, Nick."

He rose painfully to his feet and tested his bad leg with gingerly taps of his foot on the ground.

"I'll keep walking till I can't walk anymore."

Sarah removed an envelope from her jacket and handed it to him. "I want you to have this now," she said, "in case something happens and we're separated. Okay?"

He nodded and stuffed it in his pocket. She knew that it was not like Nick to ask questions, and this time it was just as well that he didn't. She did not want to share with him her fear that one of them—perhaps both of them—would not survive this day. It was a premonition, and Callahan, a man of science and logic, was not a believer in premonitions. Once she gave him the envelope she felt a strange sense of peace. She was now ready to face whatever the next stage might prove to be.

As they began to walk again, the snow crust suddenly gave way and they dropped down a small incline. Spread-eagled across the snow they struggled to get up. Callahan clutched his knee, moaning in agony. Then they looked at each other, and despite the peril of their situation, death perhaps minutes away, they both began to laugh.

"Bullocks," Callahan sputtered. "This is just fucking ridiculous."

Sarah, glancing into the distance, suddenly went quiet. Callahan followed her look. The Red Cross camp was just barely visible through the trees, perhaps no more than half a mile away.

Callahan said, "If we cut straight through to the trees, we'll be out in the open for at least ten to fifteen minutes. It's a real risk. What do you think?"

"What choice do we have?"

"None really."

Sarah said without hesitation, "Then we go for the trees."

Callahan's head snapped up and he stared at the sky. "You hear that?"

It was the sound of distant engines. They searched the landscape, trying to identify which direction the vehicles were coming from. The sound grew steadily louder, and they were frozen, pinned to the spot, listening. Then behind them, cresting a hill overlooking the snowfield, a jeep appeared followed by two trucks. In a moment Sarah recognized the Muslim warlord, riding shotgun in the jeep. The trucks were loaded with the remnants of his battered rebel troops.

Callahan said, "Let's go," and they plunged into the empty snowfield and headed, totally exposed, for the fringe of woods in the distance.

"Zigzag," Callahan shouted. "Keep moving. Stay low."

The rebels closed in and started firing indiscriminately. Callahan staggered forward, barely managing to maintain his balance, his injured leg radiating pain throughout his body. A bullet kicked up snow within feet of Sarah.

"Don't give them a target," he shouted. "Side to side . . . Broken field . . ."

They could hear the Muslim screaming at his men in Chechen.

"He's telling them to hold their fire," Callahan said, panting, struggling for each breath. "He wants me alive."

Trying to move faster, Callahan suddenly clutched his leg and collapsed in a heap. The tourniquet came loose and bloody pus oozed from the wound. Sarah quickly retied the tourniquet as he gritted his teeth against the throbbing pain.

The jeep with the trucks in its wake was speeding along the icy track, running parallel to the snowfield, and it was fishtailing wildly. Sarah helped Callahan to his feet and they stumbled forward, powered now by little more than an animal instinct for survival. Callahan started to lose his balance again, and she put her arm around his waist, trying to keep him on his feet.

"Go on," he said. "You've got to go, Sarah."

"I'm not leaving you," she shouted. "Not this time. Try! Goddamn it, Nick! We're almost there."

"I can't. Sarah—go!"

"No."

The jeep slid to a halt and the Muslim stepped down. Before the trucks even came to a full stop rebels were leaping out onto the snow, rifles drawn.

Callahan grabbed Sarah by the shoulders and looked into her eyes. "Listen to me, *listen to me now*. They don't want to kill me, they need me alive. I'm worth money to them. But if they get you they're going to rape you. Then they'll kill you. You're worth nothing to them because they can't sell you. You have to get help." He took a deep breath and continued, saying, "Run like hell for the trees." His voice was desperate, pleading.

She nodded silently, realizing that Nick was right, that this was their only chance. She kissed him hard, caught up in the urgency he was trying to convey. "I'm coming back for you," she cried as she left his side.

She pushed herself forward through the deep

snow, stumbling, falling, gasping for breath. Then rising and pushing out her legs numb with cold but moving, still moving, machinelike. "Just a little farther," she gasped. "Just a little farther, Sarah." In the distance she saw a helicopter take off from the Red Cross camp. She glanced back toward Nick and watched in horror as one of the rebels raised a rifle to his shoulder, taking aim at Callahan who was hunched over inching slowly along the icy plain. She heard the pop of gunfire and Callahan fell forward, grabbing his shoulder.

A scream caught in Sarah's throat as she took a panicked step toward him. That was when she heard the click. She stopped dead in her tracks, afraid to move, to take so much as a breath. She looked down, knowing what was beneath her feet.

A land mine . . . If she moved . . . If she took a single step . . .

"Go on, Sarah," Callahan shouted. "Go on! You can make it."

She stood still as a statue, staring at him. Numb, terrified.

"Nick," she said in a hoarse whisper. "Nick . . ."

His eyes blurred with pain, Callahan managed to get to his feet and began to hobble toward her.

"Sarah—for God's sake—*please go*. . . . " He was screaming now, his voice ragged.

Rigid with horror, she watched him come nearer and nearer. There was no choice left. The options had narrowed to one. Either she must step off the mine now or they would both die. She smiled and said softly, "I love you."

Then she stepped forward.

The blast hurled Callahan backward. He lay in the snow stunned, unable to form a single thought. He stared sightlessly into the sky. The snow started blowing, slight at first, then quickly building. He could hear the "whap-whap-whap" as the Red Cross helicopter slowly descended above him, its shadow falling across his prostrate body. A few seconds later he descended into a black void.

EPILOGUE

Two months later Nick Callahan sat in the back of a London taxi reading the letter for perhaps the tenth time.

It wasn't a long letter, but each word resonated deeply within his heart:

My sweet baby Anna, if you should ever find yourself reading this, I want you to know that I love you and Jimmy with all my heart. The man who brings you this letter is your dad. Our story is a love story, and you my darling are the happy ending. If I can't be with you, don't be afraid, you are with the sweetest kindest man I have ever known. I have loved him from the moment I met him, he gave my life meaning—most of all he gave me you. And always remember sweetheart, hold tight to Jimmy, and take care of each other and never forget what took me a lifetime to learn, you only have one heart, be true to it.

The cab pulled up in front of the town house and Callahan slowly, stiffly climbed out and stood for a moment at the curb. He took a deep breath and walked slowly toward the house. As he neared it, he heard the sound of a piano. He paused and listened. It was the theme of "Dreaming" from Schumann's *Scenes from Childhood,* and it took him back so many, many years to the abandoned church in Ethiopia and the beautiful young woman who had magically released music from an ancient, out-of-tune piano. He approached the house and through a bay window he saw the girl playing the piano. Anna. His daughter.

He limped to the door and rang the buzzer.